THE GAME OF THE SEASON

D0587361

THE GAME
OF THE SEASON

✳

HUGH DE SELINCOURT

WITH AN INTRODUCTION BY
JOHN ARLOTT

Oxford New York
OXFORD UNIVERSITY PRESS
1982

Oxford University Press, Walton Street, Oxford OX2 6DP

London Glasgow New York Toronto
Delhi Bombay Calcutta Madras Karachi
Kuala Lumpur Singapore Hong Kong Tokyo
Nairobi Dar es Salaam Cape Town
Melbourne Auckland

and associates in

Beirut Berlin Ibadan Mexico City Nicosia

Introduction © John Arlott 1982

First published by Rupert Hart-Davis 1931
First published as an Oxford University Press paperback 1982

British Library Cataloguing in Publication Data

de Selincourt, Hugh
The game of the season.—(Oxford paperbacks)
I. Title
823'.912[F]   PR6007.E6429
ISBN 0-19-281352-8

Printed in Great Britain by
Richard Clay (The Chaucer Press) Ltd.
Bungay, Suffolk

CONTENTS

INTRODUCTION
JOHN ARLOTT

The Game of the Season is a happy picture of village cricket in southern England in Edwardian times and the 1920s. It is also a period piece and an oblique, but nevertheless distinct, portrait of its author.

At least until the First World War, Hugh de Selincourt lived a life which, from the standpoint of the 1980s, must seem idyllic. Certainly the setting he grew up in was calculated to raise any young man's interest in cricket to a deep enthusiasm. Born in 1878, he grew up in a period when W. G. Grace—identified on the memorial gates at Lord's as 'The Great Cricketer'—had lifted that game to such a level that he was accepted, even by those with no interest in it, as an eminent Victorian. He went to Dulwich College, where he was a contemporary of P. G. Wodehouse and which has been long and devotedly a cricketing school. Indeed Alec Waugh recalled that he saw de Selincourt and Wodehouse playing together, under the captaincy of Conan Doyle, for the Authors against the Publishers at Lord's in 1910. At the link of the century, he moved on to University College, Oxford when such distinguished cricketers as R. E. Foster, B. J. T. Bosanquet, Harry Martyn, C. H. B. Marsham, and E. W. Dillon were regularly to be seen in The Parks.

He came down into an England under King Edward, a unique period: for those even modestly privileged, one of luxury, ease, and social acceptance. English cricket flourished. Major professionals, George Hirst, Wilfred Rhodes, Jack Hobbs, Dick Lilley, Frank Woolley, Colin Blythe, Sydney Barnes and Len Braund competed for Test places with such amateurs as Gilbert Jessop, Stanley Jackson, Ranjitsinhji, Bernard Bosanquet, Pelham Warner, Archie MacLaren, Charles Fry, Lionel Palairet, Kenneth Hutchings, Reggie Spooner, 'Tip' Foster and Johnnie Douglas. Quite irrespective of changing standards in different eras, those men provided cricket of style and character in greater profusion than England has known at any other time. For the ordinary follower it was almost a surfeit of riches.

Hugh de Selincourt did not play on that level but, in common with all who followed English sport—which, in those days, meant cricket in the summer and football (of one code or the other) in winter—he was impressed, delighted and influenced by it. On lower strata of performance, too, the game has never been healthier. This was the age of country-house cricket, perhaps the most amiable, civilized – or self-indulgent —form it ever assumed. A dozen or more cricketers, selected for their social, as well as their playing, suitability, would be bidden to some great house where they would be lodged, often for as long as a week. Readers of *Raffles* will recall how profitable he found the arrangement. Each day (often indeed there were two-day matches) a game was played on the estate pitch. The standard was high. The house party would usually consist of public school, university and, occasionally, county cricketers. Their opponents invariably included the local village, old boys' sides, perhaps a nearby town team, even MCC (at appropriate strength) and 'wandering' clubs with no ground of their own, who relied on their assorted graces and qualities for invitations to play. A few of the great country-house pavilions survived, certainly, until the Second World War.

Unmistakably Edwardian—or late Victorian—in style, red brick, gabled and plentifully windowed, they might be three storeys high. The basement was the groundsman's, with rollers, mowers, nets and assorted tools. The ground floor, where the teams normally took tea, was often used for dancing after play. On the first were the dressing-rooms and baths; the second, store-rooms and the scorers' box with a wide-window for communication with the boys who manned the scoreboard.

It was an aspect of a benignly feudal state: the most tolerant, expansive, light-hearted and pleasurable cricket man has ever known.

In those days village cricket was authentically of the village, for the simple reason that the village existed as a close entity.

The introduction of the motor cycle enabled—and tempted—the young men of the villages to the towns; and, even more decisively, the extension of the big farms, the advent of the tractor and sophisticated mechanization, reduced agricultural labour needs. As a result, the village community as it had been—that of the farms, their workers, and the services they needed—doctor, parson, blacksmith, publican and general shopkeeper—ceased to exist. The former farm cottages were snapped up, first, by commuters from the nearby towns attracted by the idea of rural peace and quiet in their free hours. Often their motor cycles went in convoy with those of the farm labourers' sons to the same town factories. Then came the weekenders, happy to buy a cheap thatched cottage to which they soon added roses—and a carriage lamp—round the door. Then the retirement age-group, to spend their last years in a quiet retreat from the towns where they had passed their early lives.

As late as 1933 the writer played in a village team of whose basic, fourteen, fairly regular players, ten had been born in the village and the others within four miles of it—though only three of the fourteen worked in the village. Hugh de Selincourt lived through that transition, though his playing days ended before it was completed.

The Tillingfold team of this book is essentially of the village: not all its members natives, but all closely linked to it. The cricket—and its players—are completely authentic. On the other hand, the genuinely funny, and often reprinted, village match in A. G. MacDonnell's *England, Their England* is not. It is a deliberately comic piece—virtually slapstick—seen from the viewpoint of the bibulous authors provided the semi-serious opposition to the village team.

Hugh de Selincourt showed in his first novel about the game—*The Cricket Match*—just how serious a matter village cricket is to villagers. Of course it is a serious business for players at all levels to the lowest except where—like J. C. Squire's 'Invalids' in the MacDonnell story—the cricketers set out to play it as farce. A village cricketer is as agonized by failure as any professional; indeed, because of lack of professional philosophy, he may feel it the more. James Barrie described *The Cricket Match* as 'the best story about cricket or any other game that was ever written'. The fact is, though, that it is not in essence a book about cricket; it is about people set against a dual background of their village and cricket. That background, though, is perfectly drawn and, as in this book, village cricket is shown in all the heart-deep gravity of those who play it.

Of course village cricket is as serious now as it ever was; only it is no longer purely of the village. It is not merely that many of the players are not natives; but that many do not identify with the village. Once the game is over when, of old, the team—and probably their opponents, too—would gather in the village pub, they tend nowadays to break up and go their separate ways. How much that is due to the fact that the earlier generation was virtually trapped by lack of transport while the men of today have cars, is a matter for conjecture.

One important quality, like the rest of village life of which it was part, was present in de Selincourt's time, but has now virtually disappeared; it was unity; call it if you will, togetherness. That quality in practice led to many village evils. People were often too close; the main weakness of village life until relatively recently was inbreeding; and it was harmful that people could not—or, equally important, felt they could not—escape from the village. In 1934, near Basingstoke in Hampshire, the writer talked with a group of seven men—engaged in haymaking—of whom only one had ever been to Southampton, thirty miles away. For good or ill, the English village as a self-contained entity ceased to exist between the two wars. For that reason alone the de Selincourt stories of Tillingfold are a valuable period piece. Anyone who plays village cricket nowadays will sense the difference when he reads them.

In *Who's Who*, Hugh de Selincourt described himself simply as 'Writer' and the remainder of the entry amply confirmed that label. It recalls, too, that his own handwriting was delicate, almost pedantic, unusual, with a positive character. He wrote most kindly to a schoolboy who sent him a letter of admiration about *The Cricket Match*. Before the First World War he was dramatic critic of the old *Star* evening newspaper; and literary critic of *The Observer*. Brother of the Oxford poetry don, Ernest de Selincourt, he contributed the chapter on 'The Successors of Spenser' to *The Cambridge History of English Literature*.

He wrote twenty-one novels; six plays and six books of what were, in his day, called *belles-lettres*, indeed that was the title of one of them. *The Cricket Match* is the only one of his works to attain any appreciable celebrity; but *The Game of the Season* and the somewhat lighter *The Saturday Match* and the two books of musings on cricket—*Over* and *Moreover*—all have their place in the canon of the work of a cricket writer of deep feeling, sharp perception and appreciable humanity.

One of his strengths is his technical understanding of the skills and mechanics of the game. It is not that of a professional player or critic, but it is penetrating beyond the usual powers of a village cricketer; and it is invariably sound. He is wise not to clog his text with technicalities, nor to talk too much shop; he does enough, however, to establish his credentials, without ever becoming pompous.

The Game of the Season, published in 1931, presumably as a follow-up to the relatively slow, but steady and convincing, growth in popularity and sales of *The Cricket Match*, which had appeared in 1924, is a collection of seven pieces woven about the theme of cricket at Tillingfold, an invented and pleasant name for a Sussex village. The first—title—piece is the strongest. It gives a charming view of country-house cricket; though on this occasion 'the General's eleven' have come out from their house party to play on the village pitch. 'Soon the ground became gay with bright blazers—an awesome spectacle to the blazerless, who mentioned in hushed voices names of clubs and schools—M.C.C.—I Zingari—Authentics—Wellington—Eton, to which these colours belonged.' Rarely in any of his cricket writing is he more a man of his period than in that sentence. There is, too, some shrewd personal observation, none sharper than of Wishfort, the manager—note, not the licensee—of the *Black Rabbit*, a passage which must surely have paid off some long-contained grievance.

As in the earlier novel, Gauvinier, the Tillingfold captain is a thinly disguised portrait of de Selincourt himself (he captained Storrington). He was, says his narrator friend in 'His Last Game'—'always a superstitious dog; not in a nice, ordinary, sensible way like most of us . . . but in his own rather peculiar way: attractive if you liked him: most annoying if you didn't . . . the beggar's always in a hurry, somehow'. After a visit to Gauvinier's house he comes away with his 'head reeling with his talk. Cricket, poetry, life, what mattered in life—money, love, affection, what *was* spiritual, what *was* material: how, in one sense, nothing mattered, how, in another, the littlest, most insignificant action might catch the light of, be the symbol of, all that was mightiest and most important'. He describes him as 'A queer fish, far too excitable, but I've always liked him.'

The plot of 'The Game of the Season' is sound; as is by no means always the case in cricket fiction. The same is true of the second story—'Tillingfold Play Wilminghurst'—and, if he has a liking for the happy ending, and for the personal success of Gauvinier, this is so honest that it is perfectly acceptable to the reader whose sympathy he elicits so unfailingly.

'How Our Village Beat the Australians' and 'How Our Village Tried to Play the Australians' are simply fantasies, light and pleasing, except when, quite unconvincingly, he draws political observation into them; he is sounder on human beings, especially those of Sussex.

In 'Tillingfold *v*. Grinling Green' and 'His Last Game' he does again what he does best, involving himself personally in the story of a game of cricket. The second of them is frankly sentimental and, in a peculiarly Gallic way, quite unselfconscious in relating the affection for, and the success of, the man who is so transparently himself. At the end 'Ours is the Real Cricket' is an amiable salute to the Sussex county cricket club, which has always adopted a paternalistic approach to its villages.

It would strain the truth to argue that *The Game of the Season* is of comparable literary merit with *The Cricket Match* but it is more than readable. The author emerges from this collection as a likeable human being: never revealing himself, his background, his class and his period more clearly than in the sentence from 'How Our Village Tried to Play the Australians': after the crowd has swarmed all over the pitch, 'Mr. Gauvinier, elated at having been at last allowed to toss and at having won it, raised his voice and appealed to the better nature of the crowd: and what man has ever made such an appeal to an English crowd in vain?'. His friendly book affords more than one glimpse of a warm, leisurely civilization which is not quite to be conjured back: though there, under the Sussex Downs, the descendants of Gauviner and his Tillingfold men still, and constantly, strive to achieve as much.

THE GAME OF THE SEASON

(*To John Ruttledge*)

PART I. PREPARATIONS FOR THE GAME

LORD! Who would get up a side? Surely no sane man. Yet here for the eighth successive season the good Gauvinier found himself let in for it again: mainly through the masterly inactivity of others. The truth was he was not sane about cricket. Mad about it, in fact, quite mad about it. He tried to find noble reasons: cricket brought all classes together; cricket was so good for the village; cricket was such fine training for youngsters. All very sound, of course, and all very true; but futile and strengthless without his own personal madness on the game, and on the game, moreover, as played on Saturday afternoons with the Tillingfold team. Such games! it was good enough.

The Selection Committee met in the billiard-room of the *Black Rabbit*. Gauvinier the Captain, Johnston the Vice-Captain, and the Secretary, who on this occasion was absent.

Johnston kept drawing lines with a pencil under a name: 'He'll be mighty sick.'

'Can't be helped: so'll seven others at least. Everyone wants to play in the General's match.'

'That's so: still . . . bit important, you know, that bloke.'

'Thinks he is!'

'That's so!'

The name underlined was Bill Wishfort, the manager of the *Black Rabbit*.

'I don't think we can do better,' said Gauvinier.

Johnston gave a deep sigh. 'All right, that goes, then.' And he slowly pushed the numbered list to Gauvinier, who was to see to its proper posting. They left the billiard-room. In the hall outside Bill Wishfort called brightly from the Private Bar: 'Just a moment!'

Johnston said hurriedly: 'Well, so long. I must be gettin' along,' and Gauvinier stepped down into the small room, where a few worthies were sitting chatting and looking through the evening papers.

'Tate's made another century, I see,' said an old cricketer in the corner.

'A lad, that!' laughed Gauvinier.

'His father, y'know, was a very fine cricketer. I played agin' him ... now what year were it? ... Sam Oxenham was a nipper, then ...'

Bill Wishfort came in smiling.

'Got a good team, skipper? I hear the General's got a real hot side.'

'Not bad, you know.'

'Might I have a look?'

'Certainly,' said Gauvinier, handing the half-sheet.

Wishfort's smile turned to a scowl as he stared at the paper. Suddenly he slammed it down on the table with a vicious bang.

'Not playin', then.'

'I'm afraid not.'

'That's the second time. I take it as a personal insult. Who's done more for the club than me? Tell me that. You name any man who's done more than me. Left out. Left out in the one game that matters.'

Gauvinier tried to soothe him.

'Well, the difficulty is, you see, you can't play in away matches and it's hardly fair to run you in for this game at home. But if anyone falls out I'll let you know straightaway.'

'It's no good talking like that. I know you've a personal down on me. The whole way the team's run and the sides picked's a bloody scandal.'

'We do our best.' Gauvinier was too old a bird to be snared into temper.

Bill Wishfort left the room on a noisy snort.

'Properly upset, he is. No mistake,' chuckled the old cricketer from his corner. 'Someone's got to stand down after all's said and done.'

'That's the side,' said Gauvinier.

The old fellow took the paper; scanned it carefully and returned it, saying:

'And not a bad one either. And you'll be needin' a good 'un, I hear. The General's got a wunnerful fast bowler

2

coming. So they say. Some relation of Mrs. Lewis. Sid and
John were speakin' of him: fair got the wind up already.
Person'ly I used to fancy a fast bowler, myself. Tire their-
selves out, y'know. You don't have to hit 'em so hard either.
Do half yer work for yer in a manner of speaking. A snick
here and a touch there. Runs don't half begin to mount up!'

'Yes; but a fast bowler on the spot . . . two or three
deadly ones early on and a side looks silly.'

Gauvinier saw one or two of the team on the way home:
each man had heard of the coming of the fast bowler, and
many stories of his feats and pace. Astonishing how rumours spread and gather force. Scott-Lewis was already loom-
ing over the game like a monstrous spectre: himself, of course,
totally unaware of the feelings his name was stirring in every
man in the village who took an interest in cricket.

Next day, Friday, the College were playing the Old Boys
on the Village Ground, so Gauvinier went down, in the
evening, to have a look at the end of the game, and give the
final touches with the groundsman to the pitch for the great
match on the morrow.

Mine host of the *Black Rabbit* was watching. A fixed glare
came over his face, his whole bearing stiffened, to show quite
clearly that a worm like Gauvinier might crawl by unnoticed
and ungreeted. However, Gauvinier ventured to walk past:
and as he passed he noticed that a man fielding for the Old
Boys was limping, as he changed over, so badly that he could
hardly put one foot to the ground: and that man, Somner,
was down on the list for the village side.

He stopped by Wishfort, saying: 'Somner can't possibly
play to-morrow. Here's our chance.'

Wishfort grew perceptibly stiffer, in surprise, no doubt,
that a creature so lowly as a worm should have a voice at all.
The thing apparently did not even notice that his company
was not wanted: behaved as if nothing had happened, as if no
fury at the vile way the Club was run existed—just as cheerful
and pleased with himself . . . Mine Host's face grew slowly an
even fiercer red in sheer disgust that such a Thing breathed at
all, let alone stood near him—him, who had done more for
the club than any man, and who was not on the list to play
to-morrow.

But Gauvinier was waiting the moment when 'over' would

3

be called. Better still, however—a wicket fell. He ran out at once to Somner.

'Sorry to see you limping like this,' he said.

'Dashed if I can put my foot to the ground,' said Somner. 'Gave me knee the very hell of a twist.'

'You ought to be careful. A knee's a tricky thing.'

'Yes. I'll give it a good rest after to-morrow.'

'I don't think you ought to play to-morrow, my dear chap.'

'Oh, rather! Hobble through all right. Wouldn't miss that game for anything, don't you know! You can shove me point and let me have a man to run for me.'

'Not good enough. Too risky for you: and there's the side to think of.'

'The side,' Somner laughed. 'It's not a county game!'

'It would be misery trying to play with a leg like that: no good to yourself or to us.'

'Look here! if you're trying to heave me out of the side, say so.'

The charm of his manner, almost Etonian in quality, disappeared. He spoke like an angry boy, jolting back his head.

'My dear man, we've got to play whole men. It's obvious you're not, with a knee like that. It's not fair on the side, and every man-jack's aching to play to-morrow.'

'Oh, chuck me out, if you want to; chuck me out.'

Gauvinier shrugged his shoulders. A college boy was making his way to the wicket.

'Am I playing or not? Because if I am not playing I shall go straight up North to-night: straight up North to-night.'

He spoke as one uttering a furious threat. Gauvinier checked himself from saying 'You can go to hell if you like,' and merely remarked:

'No; you are not fit to play.' And walked quickly back to Wishfort, thinking, as he was an optimist, that at any rate he would now make one man glad.

'Somner's knee's too badly twisted: can't play to-morrow, so there'll be a place for you all right.'

Bill Wishfort stared in front of him, preserved an icy silence, scarlet in face in his effort to make the silence more cutting. His companion on the seat seemed to be much amused. He gave him a gentle nudge with his elbow, and said gently, sitting back on the bench to swing his legs to and fro:

'Gent's speaking to you, Bill.'

Gauvinier repeated his remark.

'I shan't play!' He spoke with difficulty, as though choked with contempt for the man to whom he was speaking.

'My dear good chap!' Gauvinier expostulated. 'You told me it was the one game in the season you most wanted to play in. Of course you'll play.'

Gauvinier had long given up minding the vagaries of personal dignity: he supposed if men were young enough to play cricket, they must also remain young enough to behave as naughty little boys would like to behave, if they were allowed to.

Wishfort sat staring in front of him: his companion sitting right back, grasping the wooden bench with his hands, became almost gymnastic in appreciation of the scene.

'Shouldn't dream of playing again. I'm finished with it.'

'Go on, Bill, never give up 'ope.'

'Come on, man. It's no good cutting off your nose to spite your face. You'll be sick as mud to-morrow if you miss the game.'

'You're wasting your breath. I'm not playing. What I say, I mean.'

'Ah, don't be sore. You'll be feeling better to-morrow. The sun'll be blazing. We're sure of a piping-hot day. What-ever'll you feel like about three—when we're all in the field—the game beginning—the ground full of people watching—to think you've chucked the chance of playing? Besides, you're much too good a sportsman to bear a grudge, knowing how devilish awkward it is to pick teams.'

'Same thing last year. Left out.'

'All the more reason you should jump at the chance of playing this year.'

There was a silence, ominous but relentless. Gauvinier broke it by saying cheerfully: 'That's settled then. You'll be turning out. A jolly good job too.'

Came a reluctant growl. 'Oh, very well then. I'll play.'

'Good man. Capital!'

And there a wise man would have left it, even if he had (which is doubtful) gone so far. But there was an imp of mis-chief in Gauvinier, whose liveliness Bill's companion quick-

5

ened by his relish of the little scene, and the imp of mischief forced him to say:

'Don't look so cross, Bill. What about a nice smile, and saying, Thank you, dear Skipper, for taking all this trouble to get me the game on which my little heart was set?'

Bill's companion nearly fell off the seat backwards, rocking with joy at this new turn of the talk. Bill's lip tightened. He didn't like it. He'd never been spoken to like this before. He didn't know what to say. But something was tickling him—probably the infection of his friend's gymnastic amusement. He suddenly burst out laughing.

'Gor! if you're not the blinkin' limit. Well, thanks very much.'

His companion beat him on the back. 'Hooray for old Bill!' he called out: and Gauvinier left them struggling, as Wishfort was easing his feelings by forcing his friend backwards off the seat. Gauvinier excused himself, as he walked away, by thinking, 'Oh well, I must have *some* fun out of it,' for he knew very well that the more grotesquely a man's personal dignity exhibits itself, the more unwise it is to upset it.

Lord! who'd run a side! was the refrain in his mind, as it frequently was towards the end of any week during the summer. Strictly speaking, someone else ought to do this part of the job. Get all the ha'pence, he laughed to himself, and none of the kicks.

He entered another world with Peter Bliss, the groundsman, for whom that patch of turf known as The Square was very dear.

'Of course, some of these gentlemen who are playing tomorrow are accustomed to County Grounds, but the wicket here won't be too bad, sir, not too bad. I don't think they'll mind. Very good of them to turn out against the village. Still, they enjoy it: it's a bit of fun.'

He always spoke to one of the gentry about the gentry as one speaks of a race apart whose very presence on the Village Ground or elsewhere might be supposed to confer a blessing. Many of those addressed, who behaved as though they shared his opinion, thought him a very intelligent well-spoken fellow, a good cut above his station. Gauvinier wisely concentrated on his genuine enthusiasm for his job and put up with all the rest. Men like Peter Bliss help to foster the notion

6

that rudeness and crossness and unpleasantness imply honesty —blunt rugged British honesty. So Gauvinier smiled to think and to remember Sam Bird's favourite comment on matters terrestrial, 'It's an imperfect world, my dear sir, a most imperfect world.'

As they moved slowly along with the water-weighted roller, it appeared that Peter, too, had heard of the famous fast bowler.

'I've told the boys not to mind what they hear. So foolish, sir, isn't it, to become nervous before you've even seen the man. In a reg'lar stink, if I may say so. What the team wants is two steady opening batsmen. We've some good bats, mind you, some very pretty bats, but they've no patience to wait: to play themselves in. Too anxious to start scoring . . . Hasty.' (He shook his head and repeated) 'Hasty.'

Various members sauntered on to the ground for practice: among them came the General's butler, bright, small and out of breath—looking this way and that. He caught sight of Gauvinier and hurried up to him.

'Evening, sir. Capital finding you here. Thought I possibly might. The General—he's got twelve men—of course he could stand down himself; but I told him that would never do and I was sure you'd be glad to play twelve a-side. So many anxious to play in this game.'

'Of course. That's excellent. Twelve a-side then.'

'I'll tell him. You'll excuse my running away at once. There's the dinner, you know.'

He lowered his voice to speak of it as a high priest might of a sacrificial ceremony.

A wag among the players curled an imaginary moustache and speaking in haughty tones announced: 'Excuse me, my men, I must be strolling back home to dress for my late dinnah! . . . A chunk of bread and a lump of cheese and 'alf a pint with luck.'

There was a roar of good-natured laughter.

Gauvinier caught sight of Jimmie Marlow—a keen lad he wanted to give a game to—coming on to the ground.

He got hold of Johnston, who was among the laughers, and said: 'We'll play Jimmie, don't you think!'

'Rather! He's mad to play, I know. A real good young chap, that.'

7

'Yes, he is,' said Gauvinier, delighted to hear recognition of one of his spot boys. 'Make a cricketer, one of these days.'

And he called out to Jimmie, who, hoping against hope, came up, blushing. He had just left school and was learning to be a gardener, under Bert Tomkins, who had been a keen cricketer in his day.

'Want you to play to-morrow, Jimmie.'

''Fraid I can't, sir. My turn on the greenhouses.'

Gauvinier swore.

'P'raps Mr. Tomkins might . . .'

The boy couldn't finish the sentence. There was a silence.

'He's comin' on to the ground now. If you were to . . .'

Again the boy stopped.

'Of course! What an ass I am! I'll ask him.'

Gauvinier strode across to Bert, whom he had known for many years. They liked each other. Bert was never tired of pulling Gauvinier's leg: one joke in particular, Elizabethan in tang, concerning a hurt Gauvinier had received playing Soccer, remained perennially fresh to the good Bert.

'Evening, Bert. Looks like a fine day for the match to-morrow.'

'Wireless predicts rain in places,' answered Bert huskily.

'Old liar.'

'And serve you jolly well right if there was a good soak here. Do a lot more good, too, than you chaps are likely to do. Ah! it would that. And General's got a real fast bowler comin'! Cooh! I'll be watchin'! Shan't half laugh to meself to see your stumps flyin'! Ought to lay in a double lot, case he breaks 'em.'

'Yes, but ragging apart. We're playing twelve a-side. I want you to let young Jimmie off.'

'Ah! I don't see how I can, properly speakin'. The chaps take turn and turn about of a Saturday. It's a bit awkward-like.'

'Yes, I know, but he's mad to play.'

'And all these boys are a lot too saucy nowadays, you know.'

'You never were one to stand for a bit of fun, were you?'

'There's fun and fun,' said Bert, shaking his head very seriously. 'Still, he ain't a bad lad. I will say that much for 'im. But I don't rightly see how I can manage it.'

8

He ran through names. 'What with one thing and what with another, they has their Saturdays pretty full, and don't like changing round at the last minute like.' He became silent, pondering deeply.

'Of course, if it comes to that, there's nothing to prevent me slipping down meself before I has me tea.'

'It 'ud be devilish good of you, if you would, Bert. I'll run and tell him.'

Which Gauvinier proceeded to do, making one boy, Jimmie Marlow, tingle with happiness for many hours to come at the prospect of playing in the Great Match.

'Well, that's about all! Thank goodness!' thought Gauvinier and went home, eager as Jimmie himself for the game next day. The difficult part of the business was successfully over; there remained the jam: and a level deep red sky, glowing, promised a perfect day for the jam's savouring.

The promise was fulfilled. The morning dawned fair and still. But all was not ready yet. The 'phone bell rang. The General's butler, suavely apologetic, yet aware that a message even through his unworthy mouth, from such a being must, however subtly, confer an honour. Most upsetting for the General; but the General's best bat, a physician, sir, was called away, on an important case, so there would be no need to trouble Mr. Gauvinier to play twelve a-side.

No trouble at all, Gauvinier explained. On the contrary, he had got his twelfth man, who would be bitterly disappointed if he was robbed of his game at the last minute. Couldn't the General raise another man! No, sir, he wouldn't like even to ask him, after all the trouble he had taken, and now left without his best batsman.

'It's young Jimmie Marlow,' Gauvinier could merely moan. 'Absolutely set his heart on the game.'

'Yes, sir, I quite understand. A very pleasant lad. I'm sure he'll see how the General's placed.'

'I'll have to tell him, I suppose.'

'That would be best, sir. I'm afraid it's putting you to a lot of trouble. Then I'll tell the General you'll be playing eleven a-side as usual.'

'All right. All right.'

'Thank you, sir. Good morning.'

Lord! Who'd run a side! It was bad to scratch round to

fill the place of someone who'd dropped out. It was worse to disappoint a keen kid of his game. Cat-and-mouse sort of job. Dangling delight in front of him; then snatching it away. Black gloom took him, blackened by the fair still morning. He had no philosophy to help him grapple with a kid's disappointment. He cursed himself for not insisting on playing twelve a-side. Oh, well, it was done now. The sooner he went and told Jimmie, the sooner it would be over. Damn it! This was the sort of dirty work he simply funked. When old Bert had been so decent too about doing Jimmie's work for him!

He started his nice old car morosely and drove down into the village. He knew the back way into the vegetable garden where he would be sure to find Bert Tomkins, and took it, hoping that he would not come across the plutocratic owner of the place, who was playing for the General's team.

He peered about through the hedge of the kitchen-garden, but he had not to peer long, before Bert emerged from a potting-shed speaking intently to his second in command. Bert was on his job. And Bert on his job was another man from Bert at large: when he lolled at leisure, so far as a man of his inches might, with an air too of wary diffidence—a shy man resolved that no one shall get the better of him. Bert on his job on his own ground was assured and courteous. Gauvinier, depressed as he was, did not fail to savour, as he had often done before, the nice change in the man who came forward to greet him. He told the bad news bluntly.

'Jimmie's game's off: it's eleven a-side now. Just 'phoned through.'

He felt the sympathy in the man's grunt. But a level of feeling was touched in which neither language nor look was easy. So Bert stepped out of the gloomy silence by remarking:

'That's good. Jim's not half been set up this morning. Take him down a peg proper. Not to mention upsettin' all my arrangements, as I've told 'em I'd see to the greenhouses myself. Cricket! You chaps don't half mess things up with your cricket! Can't never make up your minds. First one thing, then another. . . . Always the same old tale.' He added in a different voice, 'I'll tell the boy. It so happens I'm goin' that way.'

'Come on, then. I'd better tell him myself.'

Bert gave Gauvinier a friendly look. They liked each other. They walked in silence to the far end of the kitchen-garden, where Jimmie was cleaning a bed. He pretended not to notice their coming.

'Bad news,' Gauvinier said. 'Rotten bad news. Just heard a man's fallen out—on the General's side. We're only playing eleven a-side.'

'Shan't be wanted, then?'

The boy's face tightened.

'Afraid not. I'm most infernally sorry.'

'Oh, it doesn't matter!'

'I'll see you get a game next Saturday.'

'Oh, it's quite all right.'

'Then you may as well do your turn here, Jim, same as usual.'

Bert spoke awfully nicely. The boy nodded. They walked away from him.

'On such a morning, too!'

'Yes. It's hard lines.'

They reached the turn into the drive and stopped. After a moment's silence Bert said: 'Well, I must be getting along,' and moved off.

Gauvinier went to his nice old car. That was done, anyhow. A beastly job. He tried not to think how young Jimmie must be feeling but knew all too well. 'Old Bert's a damned good sort!' he announced to cheer himself up. The sun began to shine again for him as he neared home. Next Saturday anyhow he'd see that Jimmie got his game. Plucky kid. Took it well.

GAUVINIER reached the gound, as the old pavilion shutters were being hoisted into position—a rather precarious operation. He missed dear John McLeod, the late Secretary, who had left the district, and had been, always, the first to arrive. Jack Evans was coming on to the ground carrying a bat he had won for the first fifty he had made in his life, made at 15, the year before. Kids were playing about, sent out to leave their parents in quiet after their Saturday dinner. No one else yet. The marquee, specially erected for this match, was up; special chairs for the General's guests in a long line; the flag flapped from the scoring-box. All was waiting, ready for the great game. Gauvinier turned slowly round, looking: a field in a lovelier setting could not be found: his eyes dwelt on the gentle line of the Downs, undulating in the distance under a shimmer of heat; on the road sloping up through the village; on the large grass circle, tightly mown: would that it were larger!

A bunch of players straggled on to the field. He ran through the side in his mind, hoping they would be punctual, as the General gave his team a superb luncheon and brought them to the ground in ample time. Two or three of his regular players (the game was an institution) were of the sort that make any game delightful simply by their quality of sheer niceness. The really good cricketer, on the ground during a game, was a unique type, hard to beat, a man at his top note, selfless, disciplined, alert; an active, potential artist. For a little while to be in the society of free happy men, under the good spell discipline imposed from within, active and unconscious; so different from the unintelligent will-less slaves, herding about like sheep under a discipline imposed from without, engendered by an incoherent mass, accumulating, of fear and prejudice.

Gauvinier pulled himself with a laugh out of the silly morass of speculation, as Johnston approached him with earnest face, wisely intent on the business in hand and on nothing in the world at all else.

'Hope we make a decent show this afternoon!' he exclaimed devoutly. 'And if you win the toss, what about putting them in, for a change? Chaps have properly got the wind up about that fast bowler. Make us look a bit silly if . . .'

'My dear man! Put 'em out in this hot sun for an hour or two—why, damn it! winning the toss to-day would be a gift, an absolute gift. They never can last, you know, these pitch-hogs!'

'Mightn't need to,' Johnston laughed.

'Oh, rot!'

'And some of 'em like to know what they've got to beat, if you take my meaning. Not me, you understand.'

'Well, we'll take what's given us, I think. Besides, we don't know that he is so very fast. You can't believe all you hear.'

'No: that's a fact you can't. Only I thought I'd mention it, you know—how chaps were feeling about it.'

'Make 'em feel different!'

'Yes. That's it!'

They both laughed, as though a little finger only had to be raised to accomplish this memorable result. The problem was left for the skipper's mind to brood over—cricket v. the nerves of the team—sense v. superstition—a nice problem: but he had yet to win the toss.

'Will you have one or two?'

He gladly accepted, but he had only had three or four when cars drove in and he went to greet the visitors.

Soon the ground became gay with bright blazers—an awesome spectacle to the blazerless, who mentioned in hushed voices names of clubs and schools—M.C.C.—I Zingari—Authentics—Wellington—Eton, to which these colours belonged. Fortunately all their unassuming wearers were not quite in full prime or full practice. But old Francis was right when he remarked in the score-box: 'Them little jackets do look nice, now. No mistake.' The visitors were a scratch side out mainly to enjoy themselves; the home-team were in desperate earnest to give a good account of themselves and to make a decent show. It mattered to them: it mattered a lot. And most of the spectators who began to wander now on to the ground in twos and threes were slowly being drawn into the same intensity of feeling: connected with the place in which they lived (though they did not often think of it), touching, too, what might be called perhaps the honour of the place (though they were not aware of ever even dreaming of that).

Gauvinier (queer artist creature sensitive to these poignant undercurrents) fought this intensity of feeling as he greeted one and another that the mere cricketer might fully emerge. Three or four strange faces, the rest familiar, and among them, praise God! all his particular favourites.

'Now then toss and get it over. And for goodness' sake win it or we shall be killed dead fielding in this blazing sun after that lunch.'

'The General does us too well. Some of us are so damned greedy. But this is a white man. If he wins the toss, he'll take pity and put us in.'

'Your cry!' laughed Gauvinier.

'Sheer manslaughter to push some of us out into this sun. Heads!'

'It's a tail.'

'Hell! That's torn it. Well. It's up to you, now. Our lives are in your hands.'

'I'd do anything to oblige, of course,' laughed Gauvinier 'But I think we'd better take first knock.'

He flung up his hands in mock despair.

'I hear you've a deadly fast bowler,' he ventured.

'Ah, Lewis. Never heard of him myself till to-day. Hope to goodness he is.'

Gauvinier went to a group of his team, who had been watching the proceedings, far less lightheartedly.

'I've won the toss,' he said.

His words were received with silent dismay. Bill Wishfort eagerly voiced their sentiments. He stepped forward and said:

'Put 'em in, Skipper. Have the sense to put 'em in.'

'Never on your life, on a day like this. Simply couldn't do it. You take my word!'

Bill could not take anybody's word, and Gauvinier quietly cursed him, as he laughed at nerves and superstitions (his own included). But Bill could not be appeased, until it was put to him bluntly that the thing was done and could not be undone. 'Sorry, but it was so obviously the right thing,' and he went off to write down the order, thinking: 'Confound it! they may simply go in now and get themselves out—who ever heard of such infernal rubbish!'

Too late anyhow to alter it now. It was a relief to explode to Sam Bird, the umpire, and hear his chuckling comment: 'Ridic'lous nonsense!' as he forced his way into his tight white coat: which done he held out his hand to have Gauvinier's wrist-watch buckled round his stout wrist which the strap just managed to encircle. He hoped, while he fitted the tiny gawd on to that burly hairiness, that he had not been high-handed and dictatorial. After all, it was their game he was running—but such an immense advantage: simply could not *not* take it when it was offered. He fumbled the little metal tongue, fixed it: hurried into the score-box: wrote down names, Charman—Booker—Johnston—Lees—himself—Jack—Phil Rogers—Wishfort—Sid. All good for a few, and Lees and Booker, especially Booker, really good bats, worth watching. And there was Booker with his pads on ready, his nice, ordinary, smiling, nervous self.

The field was being set: no man out—three slips and a third man. Yes, that must be Lewis with the ball. And here came slowly out, to keep wicket at the age of 70, John Farringdon, a member of the M.C.C. Committee, who had captained an English team to the West Indies, who had made fifty runs with a broken thumb, whose presence on any cricket field conferred an honour. You could see him being ragged about his late arrival—a little fearfully: his burly majesty, England only could have produced (and no longer does so).

Charlie Booker and Monnie Charman made their way to the wickets. What had the next minutes in store? All would soon know now the famed bowler's pace. These opening overs are too poignant a thrill. Too much depends on them. Charlie Booker was taking first ball. He is facing the dreaded bowler: not a long run anyhow—old Farringdon stoops slowly down behind the wicket. Now then! Hm—he is fast. Just a little faster than Charlie Booker has ever met—the ball misses the leg stump by inches—Charles is seconds late in his shot. The next ball short on the off appears to smack against old Farringdon's glove before Charlie makes his shot. Gauvinier's worst fears are realized. The man is really fast. If Charlie Booker can't find his pace. . . . Ah! there it is! Charles seems to wave his bat aimlessly—his middle stump is knocked clean out of the ground. Gauvinier heard Wish-fort's voice from the Pavilion: 'Simply asking for it. When we won the toss. Not puttin'' 'em in!'

o—1—o.

'Sorry,' said the returning Charles awfully nicely. 'But I never caught a glimpse like. A bit too fast for me.'

'We're for it!' said Johnston, as he hurried out to the wicket. His first ball, on his legs, he snicked for one, and long leg, seeing a chance of a run out, flung the ball but flung it wide—an overthrow was snatched amid excited cheers. The next ball hit Johnston's pads and shattered his wicket.

2—2—2.

Came Wishfort's voice of calamity. 'There you are. No use talkin' to some people! Will go there own blind silly obstinate way!' The fellow was gloating. Gauvinier could have choked him, as he buckled on his pads, fuming with slow rage. He hated the side to make no show: to be made to look silly. And Lees going in. He waved a limp bat at one. Gauvinier looked up to see his off stump tumbling out, at the next, that dreadful over's last ball.

2—3—o.

Gauvinier stripped his sweater in the score-box. The thing was taken clean out of the realm of a pleasant game of cricket on a sunny Saturday afternoon. He strode out to the wicket. Young Farringdon was bowling. Monnie played the first five balls carefully and well; the last, a slower one, he mis-judged and hit softly back into the bowler's hands.

2—4—o.

Old Farringdon, crossing over, remarked in his deep jovial voice to Gauvinier that he had seen a stand of 170 for the last wicket. 'Quite fast, Lewis,' he added.

Jack was coming in. The Captain was talking to Lewis (shaking a friendly fist towards Gauvinier), who agreed re-luctantly to take a man from short leg well in front of the wicket and put him in the deep behind the bowler. Gauvi-nier took middle and leg, thankful that inaction was at an end at last; taut, strung up, furious, he faced the bowler. The ball came, rather short on the off: he took a quick lash at it; got it in the centre of the bat: it flew high behind point, well over third man's head . . . the umpire stopped them on their third run, signalling a boundary. Third man, apparently against his will, was induced to stop in the deep.

The next ball, well up on his legs, Gauvinier played straight to the place from which short leg had been taken, hesitation between mid-on and long leg gave him two runs. The bowler, annoyed, looked towards the Captain with a sad 'You see' on his face. Oh Pharisee! The shot gave Gauvinier, knowing the bowler's feelings, greater pleasure almost than a smack out of the ground.

The next ball, a clinker, beat him all ends up and must have broken considerably, for to his astonishment his wicket remained intact.

'The bails trembled,' growled old Farringdon, beaming pleasantly, and he called out to the bowler and the field in general, 'Hit the wicket without removing the bails.'

Praise Heaven! thought Gauvinier, superstitious to his eyelids, perhaps our luck's turned. And he knew that his own luck was always extreme, dead out always or dead in. His confidence mounted to insolence, though a paltry eight runs only marked the total with four good wickets down.

Another fierce long hop on the off, the same savage slash—curse that third man on the boundary, but a quick slant-eyed look saw third man haring in, stagger back, hopelessly misjudge the curving flight of the ball and Sam Bird, staring intent, relaxed to signal a triumphant four—to the accompaniment of derisive shouts from every small boy on the ground.

'They go at an angle of forty from the straight,' growled old Farringdon—and waved a slow arm to show the immense curve the ball had taken in its flight.

'I can see the ball: my luck's in: who knows?' thought Gauvinier, with a thrill known to all at such a happy moment: felt by everyone who has played on a side; but by none so intensely as by the cricketer, for he has full deliberate time to be conscious of the thrill and to be aware of its good presence augmenting. It's more nervous work: anxiety is more biting, but the reward is incomparably greater in its actual cumulative joy.

Young Farringdon had a deceptive delivery. His action suggested a faster ball than usually came. It hung in the air and Jack, a powerful boy, a born cricketer, with a wonderful eye, fell into the trap, blundered into it head over heels, like the veriest rabbit—played at the delivery, and played feebly at that, finishing with a half-hearted scoop, the vilest cow-shot, as the ball pitched, and bounced an inch over his middle stump. Young Farringdon had the bowler's right to be over-joyed. Gauvinier, with the paternal anguish a father feels when a favourite son cuts a poor figure, was forced to remark, in palliation: 'The boy's a mass of nerves.' Young Farringdon, elated with the success of his little strategy, approached for a faster ball both in action and in run, but tossed it, at the last moment, higher and slower, making the trap more obvious: poor Jack rolled into it over and over: hit wildly, had time to recover and jab at the ball as it bounced slowly by his off stump: he was made to look and to feel ridiculous. Courteous fieldsmen hid their smiles: spectators loudly laughed. Sid Smith's kindly voice shouted clearly from the pavilion: 'Steady, Jack: watch 'em, boy.'

Gauvinier, himself a bowler, knew the ball that was coming next, simply read the meaning of the happy smile that lit young Farringdon's face: and it came; no check of the body, no last-minute stiffening of the arm, but a loosening, a quickening (very cleverly done) and the ball flew at twice its previous pace to a batsman, at last convinced that a slowish ball must come, and who made his beaten shot well after the ball had shaved his off bail. Gauvinier noticed Jack's eye flicker towards the pavilion, like some trapped animal to-wards freedom. He moved dry lips in a sickly smile. He played the next ball as though the bat were a leaden weight he had barely strength to hold: but the bat stopped the ball, and he was still in at the over's end, to young Farringdon's very natural astonishment. You could almost hear the sigh of relief from the spectators that the village pet's ordeal was passed. One murmured to another, knowing Jack's strength and skill and quickness of wrist and eye. 'It's the boy's nerves. You wait. He'll show 'em. Oh Lord! if he gets half a chance!'

There was a moment's delay. The skipper pointed out to the bowler that short leg, forgetting, was in his original place, and the bowler, reluctantly, asked him to go into the deep: with a laughing apology he ran off.

Came a growl from behind the stumps. 'These boys can't remember their places. And look at those absurd flapping hats. A little sun won't hurt 'em.'

Gauvinier noticed the two young men who roused the old man's righteous anger.

'All show!' he growled, as he tucked himself slowly down on his haunches in preparation.

Came the well-pitched-up ball on his legs, and Gauvinier played it again hard for two directly over the spot where short leg had been standing: a trick of fate to encourage the batsman and annoy any bowler living. It was more than Lewis could stand.

'I say, do you mind if we have him back?' he suggested with praiseworthy mildness to the skipper.

'No, no!' said the skipper, who knew his job backwards. 'But it's a bit risky. That beggar's got the reach of the devil and can use it.'

Back came short leg, laughing. Lewis bowled a good-length ball on the off at a furious pace: Gauvinier stepped out using all his length of reach and drove it, rather high, but hard, straight into the hands of that man in the deep if he had been there, but not being there, the hit was a safe, watched four, greeted with a roar of delight.

'Must have a man out!' the skipper remarked firmly to no one in particular and beckoned one of the slips into the deep.

But the fast bowler's cup was not yet full. The imp of chance can play mad pranks. His next ball was a clinker which flicked the edge of Gauvinier's bat, caught in two minds, and sped past the spot where the moved slip had been standing for an easy two: as nice a catch as any slip could hope for, had he been there.

'My God, what luck!' panted Gauvinier to old Farringdon, needing a breather after the sprint.

'Luck in a way. Yes,' growled old Farringdon, stoutly accurate. 'But you mucked his field up by goin' for 'em, which was the right game.'

But Gauvinier, glad as he was that he was in, was gladder still that his luck was in; and the sheer confirming good luck of his innings gave him the agreeable sensation that all the gods were fighting for him: he braced himself to control the stupidity in his batting nature which would cause even the gods themselves to fight in vain: loose feckless wipes at good-length balls: trying to bag a run where there was no run; and so forth—too long and too sorry a list to unfold at length, and one which few happy batsmen could read without a painful prick of conscience: obvious little sins against sanity which are not easy to forget.

'If only I don't get myself out: if only I don't play the fool . . .' was the trend of his prayer or thought or resolution (or rather, perhaps, a well-shaken cocktail mixture of all three).

The over ended with a one: he faced young Farringdon for the first time that afternoon, though on various other occasions he had played him and knew that if you watched him like a hawk for a bit his deceptive action ceased to deceive, became clear as a puzzle solved. Unlike the fast man, he asked to be hit, the sooner the better. 'So we'll wait a bit,' Gauvinier grinned, 'till he's a little less above himself.'

Here it came—hanging . . . hanging . . . in the air, evilly tempting: Gauvinier gripped himself, waited, played it hard and carefully back along the carpet to mid-off. Slower still, the next one, hanging worse, *wait, you fool, wait*, ah, got him: no run, though, to that cover. Look out for his fast one. No, not this: the same tossed good-length ball, dead on the wicket. No need to grip himself quite so tight: he saw it all the way: back along the carpet to the bowler. Stick to it. No hurry: no hurry. You'll get a loose one soon. But not yet. Nor the fast one, yet. Watch out for that. Again, back along the carpet to mid-off. Like a good little book. You're getting the measure. Ah, here it comes, the fast one—good length, too; full in the centre of the bat, brilliantly stopped by mid-off—a powerful drive, easily and cleanly fielded, and returned to the bowler almost in one—Gauvinier was forced to call out: 'Well fielded!'

Old Farringdon growled in huge approval: 'That's Wellington!'

It broke the queer little spell, which Gauvinier summoned back by saying to himself: 'No liberties: now, no liberties. No need to take chances with this man.'

But no chance was needed to be taken with the next ball. It was a gift, a shortish one on his body which rose to the perfect height for a hit, as hard as he liked to hit it. They ran three, as longish grass saved the four.

Jack's nerves were still mastering him, but he made one shot which might have given a keen-sighted observer some hint of what he could really do.

The clock in the village struck three: it seemed impossible that so much could have happened in hardly twenty minutes. Cars drove by whose occupants' idly turned heads seemed to say: 'So they still play cricket in the villages, then.'

Tense and eager, Gauvinier thought: 'We'll put up some sort of show yet: and make a game of it.'

Came a stinging fast one just outside his legs which he missed completely, and slapped the wicket-keeper's left-hand glove for a run; and Jack faced the swift Lewis for the first time.

'Of course a straight one with Jack as he is,' but it went just outside the off stump. The bowler wiped his face and neck with a handkerchief: he was beginning to feel the sun, which was very hot. He must have got his hand wet, for the next ball slipped out a full toss straight at Jack's body: obvious danger steadied the boy's nerves, and for the first time he showed something of his quality by standing firm as a rock and hitting it full and clean and effortlessly to the boundary amid a roar of joy from his supporters.

'God! I was afraid I'd killed him!' Gauvinier heard Lewis remark to old Sam Bird, who fatly grinned and shifted slowly on his feet.

He's not right yet, thought Gauvinier as Jack was badly late for the next ball and was within inches of being bowled by the one that followed; but the boy was clearly getting himself in hand if only he could survive for another over or two. The last ball was short on the off; Jack lashed savagely at it, hit it hard and full, straight towards the large-hatted cover, who was startled, stepped on one side, shoved out a stiffish arm and ran after the ball flipping bruised fingers. Not a good exhibition of fielding; but nothing could have improved upon his apology; for on regaining his place he sang out in a beautiful clear voice:

'I am so sorry, but my beastly hat flapped in front of my eyes.'

Old Farringdon growled a few apt words that would burn any paper on which they were printed.

While Gauvinier recovered his wind he listened to a growled homily on a certain school which turned out an article in the shape of young men who were all show and no good: from one whom no institution could have turned a hair's breadth from his own nature's course—not even a public school, and yet the very epitome of every public school. Odd that a nation that produced the extreme individualist—poets, heretics, buccaneers and explorers—should have evolved the most perfect system for turning men out to pattern, trained to regard any divergence from that pattern with suspicion. But they were putting thirty up on the board: slowly the game was being pulled round. Over was called, and young Farringdon prepared to bowl to an obvious victim with cheerful confidence. Too cheerful. Jack was himself. He played the ball back to mid-on, making it look an easy one and the delivery guileless and stiff: the whole thing, indeed, obvious and simple as a solved anagram. The bowler refused to notice the difference, though it became clearer with every ball Jack played: for it is difficult to realize, when you've as good as bowled a man with every ball you've given him, that your bowling has ceased to trouble him much: but it was fairly obvious by the end of the over (maiden as it was) to everyone else on the ground.

'Humph!' grunted old Farringdon in approval. 'He can bat a bit, that youngster!'

Somehow, Gauvinier felt, the side had got ditched at the start like a car—in rather a large, deep, mud-bottomed ditch, too, at the start of a day's run. It was backing well on to the road again, now: no serious damage done: they'd have a run for their money yet and make a day of it. The sting was leaving the fast bowler's pace. He'd morally sent both batsmen back to the pavilion: yet there they were, more and more at home at the wicket: and the sun was not getting cooler. Three runs came that over, and no ball looked at all dangerous. His vision of a startling analysis began to fade.

The game had reached the tug-of-war stage, where both sides hold on and grimly pull; there is little movement; only the tautness of the rope and the stretched stillness exist to mark the intensity of the contest.

Gauvinier adjured the impatience in him to wait for the loose one. And both bowlers, aware of the crucial point the game had reached, gave no run away and fought for the huge advantage the fall of a wicket would give them.

Jack was playing now with quiet confidence, as though the shy weakling's place had been taken by a strong experienced batsman. And the score was creeping slowly up towards forty—a bye, a run, a leg-bye: and then a short run to cover, who still wore the umbrageous hat, excited the fieldsman so that he returned the ball wildly, and to old Farringdon's growled rage, presented Tillingfold with two runs. A little thing, but important at that tense moment. Young Farringdon, the bowler, was annoyed and pitched his next ball just that little bit too far up that turns a good-length ball into a half volley and Gauvinier, rejoicing, swept it for a pleasant four.

It was the last ball of the over. Jack played Lewis's first three beautifully, then took a rash bang at the fourth, which soared spinning towards third man, who to Gauvinier's dismay was judging it perfectly this time: the ball fell right into his hands and fell right through them, so slowly dropping that he made a frantic grab at the falling ball. He'd stroked his brilliantined hair with his hands . . . must have; Gauvinier thought in his exuberant thankfulness: while the field rang with yells of derisive triumph.

From that moment the character of the game entirely changed. No trace now, except in memory, of the ditched car: no hint of the grim tug-of-war. Tillingfold seemed out for a joy ride, after all, though they'd started late.

'Whatever the pace, a half-volley remains a half-volley,' thought Gauvinier as he savagely drove the next ball to the boundary—which the man in the deep fell over in his failure to reach. Runs came at a pace. They were nearing sixty, when Gauvinier saw the old Captain approach Lewis and heard him suggest a rest. The new bowler could not find his length: a long hop, a full toss—a kind gift of three to each batsman—all run, Gauvinier happily cursed, panting. There was not a dry inch on his shirt: his forehead dripped, his hands were wet with sweat, and he wouldn't have changed places with any man alive. His chief thought now became to keep his hands dry enough to hold the bat.

Sixty went up. Young Farringdon, who had been bowling very steadily, was taken off. The pace became fast and furious: (seventy went up) too fast for Gauvinier—who, still panting from a hard-run three, took a mighty dip to make sure of the six such a ball promised, mishit and skied it and the deep field, running at full speed, brought off a beautiful catch.

Gauvinier, wet in body, dry in mouth and throat, hot as he was happy, and happy as he was hot, rejoiced to remember that the good Mrs. Peckham dispensed lemonade at 2d. a tumbler. He gulped down two, before he was in a normal state to enjoy two more with a friend. Then lighted a cigarette, pleased at his restraint in stopping at four. The cigarette did not taste bad, as he listened, too sweating hot to blush, to nice remarks on the value of his knock, and watched Bill Wishfort with his pads on proudly vociferous and thankful that he had persuaded a timorous skipper to take the advantage of first knock.

Phil Rogers was in, a reckless hitter with a marvellous eye, young and strong: not one to need a breather after running three. He and Jack were good pals: and they enjoyed stealing runs almost as much as hitting fours. The two were famed for this, and at the first short run, every small boy yelled with delight at the sure prospect of seeing some fun. The fun was there, all right. The field, already a little rattled, became wild: and Phil's luck was in. Jack called for a foolish run (even though Phil was backing up half-way across the pitch), the boy from Wellington picked it up neatly and flung it at the wicket, which he missed by inches, and the ball went for four overthrows, sending up the hundred, to a roar of applause.

Kind heaven! How those two boys enjoyed themselves! and all the side with them in an exaltation which spread to every spectator on the ground and touched even the visitors who were beginning to arrive in their best frocks for polite conversation and tea.

Phil and Jack hit like kicking mules and ran like greyhounds, with that instant understanding that becomes the despair of fieldsmen.

110—120—130 went up, and a steadier, longer round of applause, in which the visiting side joined to a man, announced that Jack had made his fifty. Phil had been getting the lion's share of the bowling, but now Jack had pretty well all of the next three overs, in which he took his score past eighty with the help of a new bowler whom he beat unmercifully, Gauvinier marvelling why Lewis, who must surely be rested, was not given another chance.

The last thing that anyone imagined possible then happened and a wicket fell. Phil Rogers drove the ball hard to mid-off, and the Wellington boy jumping neatly to one side brought off a brilliant catch with his left hand.

164—6—36.

Bill Wishfort went beaming out to carry on the good work. The fast bowler, Lewis, by his gestures appeared to be explaining to the captain that he had strained his arm throwing: perhaps that was why Bill waved to his supporters from the wicket. He was not a very good batsman, but he could hit a ball hard on his day; and this was his day: he made sixteen in twenty minutes, while Jack, to everyone's tense excitement, was getting very near his century.

192—7—16.

'Don't you blokes let him know. Make him nervous as a monkey,' said Sid Smith, as he hurried out, chewing his usual bit of grass.

'I'll declare when he makes his hundred and we'll have tea,' said Gauvinier, for the first time in his life perhaps wishing that there were no tea interval.

Roars of joy broke out as Jack made a magnificent pull for four.

This damned tea-party stuff takes such a time. Gauvinier was torn to pieces. Hardly two hours to get 'em out in. Wasn't enough. Five more the boy wanted. Oh good, there came two more of them: and a leg-bye snatched by Sid gave him the bowling again. This must be last over. It was. Jack ran out at the first ball and hit it clean into the road for six, sending up the 200 and making his own century in one glorious smack, which everyone applauded wildly. Nor was he finished with it. The next ball but one he drove for four and the last (oh so rightly!) he lifted out of the ground, on which the innings was instantly declared closed, at 215 for 7, Jack Evans not out 113.

Tillingfold were pleased to make a hundred in an afternoon: this, incredibly after such a start against such a side, was their record score. The whole team walked down to the marquee for tea in a sort of elated swoon, the men who had failed, the men who had not failed and the men who had not batted at all, happy in the side's success.

The old skipper shook his head at Gauvinier, his eyes twinkling: 'Shouldn't have done it! Pushing us out into that hot glare. Butchery. Massacre. A shambles.' He leaned nearer: the banter went out of his voice: 'Marvellous game! Cricket. Who would ever believe after those first ten minutes that we were in for this? It was a fair bet you wouldn't make twenty, let alone 200. I've played a good many thousand games of cricket, but I doubt if I've ever seen such a complete change—ever.'

Half Gauvinier's mind was listening: half was thinking that if they got a move on with this tea business, there would be two good hours' play, and every available minute was wanted and wanted badly. One thing he knew by experience; there was something about these swift afternoon games that made sitting on the splice almost impossible: even without the temptation of Sid Smith's bowling; one of the few real old countrymen remaining in village cricket. He looked innocuously simple: yet what he didn't know about bowling wasn't really worth knowing: three steps casual run, an easy swing and no two balls were flighted quite alike. Moreover, his habit of lovingly chewing a bit of grass and wearing a collarless shirt helped to blind many an experienced club-batsman to the skilled guile his rustic nonchalance concealed. He had not yet done himself justice in the General's match: he was inclined to be overawed by those little jackets: but just a turn of the wheel of chance in his boyhood and every cricketer in the world might have known his name. It was all there: though he was born to blush unseen, a mute inglorious George Cox, upon the Village Green.

Sid Smith was strongly attached to Jack Evans, whom he had spotted as a cricketer in long clothes and trained as a cricketer as soon as he could toddle. And now at tea he was exulting in the boy's success, who what with his long innings and Sid's remarks remained a silent peony, industriously absorbing tea.

Sid's job during the week was about the dullest job a man could have: now all his pent-up power of enjoyment throve and flourished. He was himself, happy and unhampered—a good sight. Laughter and loud talk filled the hot marquee whose canvas sides flapped lazily in the heat. Most of the visitors were taking tea outside. Bill Wishfort's voice rose clear above the rest. He was actually being useful, urging them to finish up tea and get on with it. Peter Bliss was pulling the roller off the pitch. Sam Bird muttered a protest that Bill had not been standing umpire in the sun for two hours.

Gauvinier rose, laughing. The General, kindest of hosts, entered, beaming, with packets of cigarettes, anxious that his ices should be properly sampled by his guests. 'The ices, Mrs. Peckham, the ices. These gentlemen . . . Such a day too. Just the day for ices. . . .' (They were being swiftly handed round in saucers.)

'Put our eyes out, sir.'

'Oh rubbish, rubbish! And Jack, not have an ice after such an exhibition of battin'! Absurd. Eh, Jack!'

Jack sputtered: 'Yessir!'

'Give you a bat for makin' a century. Capital.' He leaned over the boy's shoulder and whispered, 'A bit shaky at the start though, weren't we!'

Jack sputtered: 'Yessir!' gulping ice.

'Never mind. Never mind. We finished in a canter. What? And a miss is as good as a mile. Ices! Ices! Of course you must have ices. Have some more!'

The teams' throats ached with the cold wolfed ices: Gauvinier hoped their stomachs wouldn't, thankful to notice Johnston well on his way to the pavilion to put on pads and gloves for keeping wicket, and Sam Bird leaving the marquee.

The General's opening batsmen were waiting, ready. Two good hours to get the side out. It could be done. They had some hurricane hitters. If they got really going! Won on time. That, too, could be done. But time now was the main enemy. They had the clock to beat.

At last they were in the field: every man, alert, on his toes, resolved to snap up any chance that came his way. Sid Smith opened the bowling: no ghost of nervousness hovered over either batsman. They knew what they wanted to do and did it, taking no risks, watching Sid carefully as he deserved to be watched.

Good sound cricket: no loose balls: no wild shots: no slack fielding. Gauvinier bowled the other end: and met the same sure, confident batting, with runs scored by shots not commonly seen on the ground. Two overs each were bowled in this way: you knew the batsmen had started out confidently to get the measure of the bowling, master it and then force the pace. They were doing it, too: no sign of a chance; no hint of difficulty with any ball. They began to open out: a huge

27

clean hit off Gauvinier's bowling past Jack Evans at deep mid-wicket, one for the throw, they agreed as they passed—but they reckoned without Jack, who picked it up and threw it in at a terrific pace, first bounce over the wicket, to Gauvinier, who snapped off the bails before the astonished batsman could quicken his pace from the centre of the pitch. He had not even looked in Jack's direction, the second run seemed so easy and so certain. The throw would have been remarkable on any ground in the kingdom, for pace and straightness, a superb piece of fielding.

28—1—16.

The new man was a stranger—McClintock by name—with a big reputation: he had been making a lot of runs for one of the minor counties: a tall lithe man with a very bright eye and an extraordinarily nice smile. He came in, smiling: and watched Gauvinier deliver the last ball of his over, from which the first semblance of a chance was given; for it cocked up just out of Gauvinier's reach, though he flung himself at it. 'You got within inches; I shouldn't have thought you could have got within yards,' McClintock remarked.

Gauvinier liked him immensely for his way of making the remark; which did not prevent him from praying devoutly that the delightful fellow might underrate Sid Smith, who had just picked himself another bit of grass.

Jack had come in to cover from deep mid-wicket. The first ball came hard along the ground in his direction.

McClintock shouted 'Wait!' in the nick of time, for Jack reached it on a running dive.

'That boy can field!'

He took a mighty dip at Sid's tossed-up slow one, missed it, barely escaped being stumped. Sid grinned. He began a hit at the next one, checked himself, and blocked it, laughing, almost on the run. Sid grinned more widely and waved his deep fieldsmen right back on to the boundary. Not far enough. For the next ball thumped plump down on the marquee—a clean swift tremendous hit—one of the best ever seen on the ground.

Old Sid swallowed the bit of grass he was chewing. He didn't much like that. A slightly slower, tossed a little higher, well up on the leg stump. Would he hit across it? fall into the old trap, this blazered toff, same as Bill Marnock or Joe

Smith! Lor' lumme, look. Yes, he's missed it. Yes, gently knocked the bail off—Sid Smith leaned staring forward, as though hardly believing his eyes—then suddenly stamped and flung his cloth cap on the gound (the first time Gauvinier had ever seen him do it) mad with delight, and yells of joy broke out from the village spectators in approval of their beloved Sid. Gauvinier came beaming up to him: 'Well *bowled*, Sid!' And Sid Smith announced with fervour: 'I'd rather have had that bloke's wicket than be give a hundred quid!' and he shook his head slowly from side to side to show how absolutely he meant what he said.

Young Farringdon came in next, annoyed at McClintock's downfall.

'Damn silly, I call it, to chuck your wicket away,' he said to Sam Bird, who cordially agreed. He did not follow the bad example: indeed he went perhaps a little too far in the opposite direction—towards over-caution: for he felt wistfully at the first ball and missed it: watched the next like a wary panther to the last moment and tipped it gently off the edge of his bat into Gauvinier's hands at short slip.

The incident had a curious effect upon Sam Bird, whose standard of an umpire's dignity was high. He announced as he advanced to the wicket, 'And the ball, gentlemen, is over,' and slowly bent up his burly form in massive silent mirth. He straightened himself to say with purple face in a hoarse voice: 'Good as a play!' and once more bent as far double as his bulk permitted, murmuring: 'Damn silly, I call it,' and heaved himself upright to add: 'There's more ways of bein' silly than one!' and wheezed.

Suddenly he recollected himself; his manner completely changed and he said very seriously: 'Extremely well bowled, Sid. Useful men to see the back of and you had 'em both guessin'.'

The young man with the perfect manner who had fielded in a too-large hat came in: but he had left his too-large hat behind him. Sid and Gauvinier exchanged glances which said distinctly how each longed to have a go at him. The innings was not going according to the batting side's plan, checked suddenly by Jack's amazing throw just as they were settling down to start lapping, opened full out, on top. But the game was far less over than many seemed to think, who did not

29

know the side. No. 1 (the boy from Wellington) was going strong, and taking no chances, and Gauvinier knew of three men who were good for any amount on their day; and only two who were negligible but would have to be got out. A neat two to leg was the only score from that over.

Gauvinier could see old Sid quite scratching himself he so itched to have his go at the little lady-lardy-da chap, and it was obviously a nasty surprise to find his feeling most courteously reciprocated. He played the first ball with careful vigour; and there was no girlish fumbling, no coy uncertainty about his next shot, which, beautifully timed, swept the ball out of the ground, curving over Sam Bird's head. Old Sid was considerably rattled, and put down his first bad ball, a short one on the leg, which was banged against the pavilion for four. Nothing reckless either about him: he played the last three balls as they deserved, correctly: but he had quietly, without the shadow of a risk, helped himself to ten, and showed every sign of intending to help himself to a good many more. It was as though he had applied a quick relentless sponge to the happy figuring on Tillingfold's little slate. Every scrap of their skill and energy was still needed and urgently with men like this to beat, and TIME with every minute coming to their aid.

The game took on a fresh intensity, wound more tightly up by the fact that the batsmen had obviously batted together before and also knew how to run: backing up to the very limit, and across the pitch in a smooth flash.

Short safe runs were applauded, and brilliant bits of fielding. Gauvinier kept changing the bowling, but the hundred went up at a good level pace. Unless a wicket fell soon the clock must win; and just possibly a victory might be snatched with a bout of furious hurricane hitting.

Gauvinier went on again himself. Keyed up too tight he bowled his fastest ball, and with an inward curse saw it was too short, saw the quick wristy lash of No. 1, saw the ball whizz off —and Jack running fifteen yards over roughish ground reach it and bring off a perfectly judged catch, shoulder high—the ball travelling at a vicious pace.

An hour to go, and four good wickets down. No dawdling either: the incoming batsman—good man!—passed the outgoer ten yards and more from the pavilion. Little excellent courtesies like that add immeasurably to the quality of a game. The batsman was sobered by his partner's misfortune: the bowler, a little above himself, sent down a beauty which the young man was glad to stop: the next one was of the same brand, a shade faster, and came a shade quicker off the pitch: hit the edge of his bat high up, shot off towards Sid Smith at short slip, who lurched forward and brought off a snappy catch in his enormous right hand.

Five good wickets down. Again the whole character of the game had changed like a turned page: and the old skipper came hurrying roundly in—the very devil of a man to dislodge: but both men had to play themselves in.

He cut his first ball hard to Bill Wishfort at point, who earned a shout of applause by jumping to stop it; and fearfully pleased was Bill that he'd managed to get to it.

'Shows how they're all on their toes,' thought Gauvinier beaming, 'if Old Bill's caught the infection to be as nippy as that.'

He put on Sid Smith, thoroughly rested, at the other end. 'No good my trying to sit on the splice,' laughed the newcomer, Paget-Wilson, to Gauvinier, as he took centre. 'Leave that to old Farringdon, who's saved more games than I've played in.'

He was tall and well made: the sort of man whose presence on a side goes far to make any game enjoyable: incidentally, as Gauvinier knew, a first-class cricketer, but out of practice: only played two or three games now every summer. If he got going he could hit as hard and as clean and as often as V. T. Hill. The uncertainty of his form made the tense excitement feverish. Sid Smith knew him of old: and his jaws tightened grimly on his bit of grass. He reached out with quick little steps and smothered the first ball neatly back to the bowler. Curious fellow, he seemed unable to make any movement unexpressive of gaiety and good nature: a man harmonious as a squirrel. And old Sid bowling to him—playing the same game, wearing the same clothes (except for turned-down inches missing from his shirt); a man, too, and a very nice man, yet as different in everything but shape and appearance as a squirrel from a mouse or a mole. Oh Lord! to give play to the rich, to the infinite variety . . .

The same shot, harder—no short runs possible, though,

and the old skipper hated his girth and age—game old boy to be playing at all, facing up to his encroaching disabilities with a laugh. 'Hit fours, Willie, and spare my wind!'

And hang it! look at that! Sid, wanting to lure him farther out, tossed up a shorter one, and the guile failed, for Paget-Wilson waited, stepped back and with a quick neat pat sent it skimming to the long-leg boundary, far from any fieldsman.

'Always obey a good skipper,' he laughed.

After that shot he attacked every ball: not wild hitting by any means, but the ordinary forward shot made mid-off or mid-on sit up. By quick foot-work, too, he turned many a good-length ball into a half-volley and drove it. In a quarter of an hour he had put on 35, when Sid caught him at last in two minds and he skied a huge hit straight into the hands of Booker in the deep, who held it—by the time P.-W. was turning for his second run.

'Coo! I enjoyed that knock!' he said to Gauvinier, drawn from short slip half-way up the pitch in sheer excitement.

And every one else on the field had enjoyed it, too; enjoyed also its perfect close.

Only the clock to beat now—Time, who was dealing relentlessly with the burly majesty of old Farringdon cheered and clapped (so rightly!) as he made his slow brave way to the wicket, though no one knew this was to be his last appearance.

Another change came over the spirit of the game. The fieldsmen drew nearer in from the deep. They wouldn't have done that a few years ago. He played his first ball a little wide of cover: no run now, for him who had been noted for quick running between wickets, a perfect judge of a run.

'Damn nuisance being old,' he growled with a smile.

And most men wished, with varying degrees of awareness, to be as game as he, if they reached his age.

For nearly a quarter of an hour the two batted safely and well; time, it seemed, their enemy, was for a little while on their side, to save the game; when Gauvinier caught and bowled the skipper from one that popped up at the last moment. Seven wickets down: only Lewis the fast bowler—and the General himself and Bert Tomkins' plutocratic employer, none of whom were cricketers.

It all depends on how that fellow Lewis shapes, thought

Gauvinier, at the last pitch of excitement: and no one in Tillingfold had the chance to know how the dreaded bowler shaped, because Gauvinier knocked his off stump out of the ground first ball.

Old Farringdon was still there—'saved more matches than I've played in'; and he showed every intention of remaining there. He played five balls of Sid's over with unwavering confidence, and cleverly put the last ball to leg, deliberately bagging the bowling. Bert Tomkins' Boss, more at home in Lombard or Threadneedle Street than on a cricket ground, and more alive to the niceties of the money market than to the niceties of the game of cricket, felt he was entitled to a smack or two after fielding all the afternoon in the hot sun. He was quite unable to appreciate old Farringdon's skill and intention. He amused Gauvinier by remarking: 'The old boy seems to want all the bowling.' Forgivingly, as a man would who is quite able to look out for himself.

Gauvinier bowled: Farringdon played it on to his pads, and off towards leg.

'Come on: come on!' cried out the financier in tones of authority, pacing down the pitch.

'Stay where you are!' shouted old Farringdon, furious.

But he didn't: he hurried on, cheerfully calling, and old Farringdon started off—to be run out, easily, yards outside the crease.

'So sorry: but there'd have been a run if you'd started at once,' Bert Tomkins' Boss called out with perfect assurance.

No one heard old Farringdon's growled remarks, after his formal acceptance of all blame.

And only the General now remained, with only two or three more overs possible. It was clear that the financier had long forgotten in more serious pursuits what little cricket he may have known. He wobbled his bat about, miraculously stopping a straight one, having his wicket shaved—and then the bad thing happened.

For the last ball of the over Gauvinier sent down a slow yorker on the middle stump. Misjudging the pace the batsman overbalanced and stumbled, bat and legs towards point: not a stroke at all but a scramble.

'How's that?' yelled Gauvinier. Up went Sam Bird's hand.

'Ah, my dear fellow! I hit the ball with my bat.'

33

'Off your foot,' said Gauvinier shortly.

Bill Wishfort, full of zeal, hurried forward from point, eager to assert himself and get a little of his own back.

'He played the ball hard to me. We don't want to win like that. Use your right as captain to reverse the decision.'

'Oh no. Mistakes will happen. I was given out,' he spoke like a pleasant martyr.

Gauvinier turned on his heel without a word and walked towards the pavilion cursing to himself: 'Damned if I let down old Sam Bird,' and positive the fellow had kicked the ball on to his bat.

Paget-Wilson came up to him.

'Isn't it muck, that sort of thing? You should have heard old Farringdon on his run out! One of the best games we've had though. Quite one of the best.'

'Too damned like life!' laughed Gauvinier, soothed but sore. 'But as Sam says, "It's an imperfect world, sir, it's an imperfect world."'

But the imperfect world contained pints of old ale at the pub, and old Francis, the scorer, to drink them with, and another friend or two, while Tillingfold's worst start and biggest victory were broodingly discussed.

TILLINGFOLD PLAY WILMINGHURST

(To Joe Page)

GAUVINIER'S experience in running the Tillingfold side for some years had led him to pay small heed to any bad preliminary rumours as to the composition of the Saturday team. The list was posted in the village on Thursday evening, and unless he had official information that a man could not turn out, he left it at that.

As in all clubs, of course, on some Saturdays eighteen Tillingfold men were keen for a game, on others eight: and on the latter occasions men who groused to the effect that they were never asked to play invariably had a prior engagement or grumblingly consented to 'make one,' inferring, as was often painfully true, that they would not have been asked if anyone else had been available. Getting up a side is no easier at Tillingfold than it is elsewhere, but the games which Tillingfold played were better games than he had ever played elsewhere.

The ride to the ground or to the conveyance that was to take the team from the village square to the opponents' ground was always an anxious ride for the good Gauvinier, skipper of the Tillingfold eleven.

The ride was more anxious than usual this Saturday, when Tillingfold were playing Wilminghurst, pet opponents, with whom many close battles had been fought in past seasons. Two good men were genuinely unable to play: the team's best bowler was seedy but would turn out if he could. Report credited Wilminghurst with a specially hot side.

No one was about in the square. The conveyance waited dolefully empty. Old John Meadows limping by to the 'pub' smiled to Gauvinier: 'Got to scratch the match, I hear.' He had played for Tillingfold forty years ago and did not approve of the way the young fellows went on nowadays: 'what with motor-cycles, pickchers and sech.'

'Oh, I hope not!' Gauvinier answered.

'Can't raise a side, I'm told,' the old fellow continued gleefully.

'Oh, we'll do that all right if we have to rope in the chaps from the Union.'

'Ah, things ain't what they was: not by a long chalk.'

Gauvinier turned away to meet Tom Rutherford, slow bowler, staunch cricketer, who had spent many years in Tasmania, and advocated in a gentle undertone drastic measures with slackers and grousers.

'Got a side?' he asked.

'Don't know yet!'

'Not going to scratch?' he inquired.

'Scratch!' snapped Gauvinier.

They both laughed. Then went through the side: Eight men and a boy were certainties and among the men were two the mention of whose names caused bitter mirth to the friends.

'We're in for the deuce of a hiding.'

'Damn good job, too.'

Sam Bird, the umpire, trod softly into the square, careful not to jolt himself or to stamp holes in the road with his bulk. He announced like a conspirator, smiling at a secret joke:

'I'm told Mr. Marling is playing for Wilminghurst.' He surveyed the sky with beady eyes and addressed it. 'Saw he made ninety-one for 'Orsam against Littlehampton t'other day in twenty-three minutes.'

But Sam Bird could not remain disheartening: his devotion to Tillingfold cricket and the Tillingfold skipper was deep and unshakable.

'However,' he said slowly, tapping the words out with a fat finger on Gauvinier's coat, 'at cricket—you—never—know. Never.'

Eight men and a boy, Gauvinier was grimly thinking; it would be the first time in seven seasons he had come on the field without a full side. Nice thing, Tillingfold turning out short!

It was not a cheery team that left the village square at 1·58 for their Saturday afternoon sport. 'A bloomin' funeral, more like,' as one man put it.

Arrived, they straggled sadly over the field to the pavilion in the far corner of the ground. It was obvious that Wilminghurst had got a hot side, even before their captain Southernhay's bright asseveration of the fact to Gauvinier, who was in the mood to find him disgustingly sympathetic. 'What a pity! It does spoil a game so, doesn't it, when one side is too vastly superior?'

'Oh, we're not beaten yet!' laughed Gauvinier.

'Marling's turned out for us. Hit up ninety-one . . .'

'Yes, I know. Let's toss.'

'Ninety-one in twenty-three minutes is pretty good going. And this ground's faster. You cry.'

'Heads.'

'It is.'

'You bat first.'

It was the first time Gauvinier had ever put opponents in as the result of sheer cowardice. In their present mood his men were not good for twenty runs. But he felt guilty and ashamed.

'Come on!' he told them in the visitors' room. 'I've put 'em in! We'll get 'em on the run! Then knock off the runs.'

'Some 'opes!' was chorused.

He did not stop to argue, but hurried out to tackle the unpleasant job of asking for a substitute. For two he could not bring himself to ask.

Hardly a catch was flung from one to another as the team (eight men, a boy, and a substitute) proceeded sadly into the field, followed closely by Marling, the cheeriest soul who ever gripped a bat handle, chatting and laughing with Southernhay, obviously awed at opening the innings in such brilliant company. Marling took middle and leg, made his block with two rapid little taps and stood up, twiddling his bat round, surveying the field with a confident beam that meant business.

Gauvinier took the first over; keen as Lucifer to get a quick wicket, knowing well how shaky Marling could be before he felt the ball clean and hard upon his bat. Gauvinier was mad to begin the game; once in it, all odious preliminaries were immediately forgotten. There was something to bite into, something good and solid. But he was in for a penitential half-hour, which he vaguely sensed as he eyed his placed field for the last time—three men who were safe to hold a catch, two real good triers, the rest . . . oh, well, it was decent of them to turn out at all, especially when one remembered how devilishly hard a cricket ball must seem to them. Gauvinier bowled medium-fast, using his height well. His first ball

Marling played out to freely and returned to him at a fair pace along the carpet; his second ball beat Marling and came within a couple of inches of the off bail. The wicket-keeper grinned cheerfully as he lobbed the ball back, wagging his head to one side knowingly. Gauvinier was so braced that he felt no annoyance to hear mid-off, whose fielding was a calamity, draw attention to his presence by remarking. 'That's the stuff to give the troops.'

The third ball struck the edge of Marling's bat and flew straight at short slip, who stumbled back as he saw it coming, stumbled forward as the ball smacked into his large hands, and fell, dropping as easy a catch as short slip will ever have in this wicked world where no catch at short slip is really easy. Gauvinier forced a grin upon his face, forced a shout of 'Bad luck' from his lips to the sorry fieldsman, and turned to deliver his next ball, with black fury boiling through his veins. A yorker: you could see the wicket shake as it shaved the leg stump and went for two byes, which Marling picked himself up to run, after his huge missed effort to wipe a full toss out of the ground.

Gauvinier was not consoled by Marling's kindly remark: 'A squeak, that! Your luck's well out!'

The gay batsman could stand no more of this nonsense: the next ball he drove hard—a lovely shot, bang against the wooden pavilion, terrifying mid-off by his proximity to its flight.

Gauvinier curbed his bitter wish to say how wise it was not to have put a hand out at that one: might possibly have stopped it. He listened without a word to mid-off's remark that he appreciated a good hit when an opponent made it; he was, at any rate, a true sportsman in speech, whatever his more practical deficiencies might be. The last ball of the over was a slower one, which Marling, slightly mistiming, lifted towards Jenkins in the deep. Gauvinier had a vivid imagination, but he never imagined for an instant that the good Jenkins would hold such a catch. He had to walk three steps forward and wait for the ball to fall into his hands: instead of which Jenkins, pleased with himself for noticing that it was a catch at all, ran back, shouting, 'That's mine,' then, like a wounded bird, hurried to the right, then to the left, and finally dashing forward as the ball fell, stumbled on to his hands.

He got up, walked leisurely after the ball, flipping his stung hand, found it and hurled it in, furious and convinced that the catch was well out of his reach.

During these manœuvres the batsmen had run three, and Marling, with a laughing apology for bagging the bowling, faced the fastish but erratic Longman, who took three little steps to the wicket and delivered the ball with the unexpected suddenness of a catapult. An early success inspired him. On his day he could be deadly, and Gauvinier hoped this might be his day: he hoped it very much, but Longman's first ball was a hot long hop, shoulder high, which Marling hit out of the ground for six.

'I like them,' he remarked to the wicket-keeper, while the wall was climbed and the ball retrieved.

Poor Longman found the wait of an inordinate length. He stood on fire with his blush, silently watching the man climb back over the wall to his place. Longman's second ball was also short, on the off, and beaten past cover to the boundary: his third was driven for two; his fourth went somewhere near the wicket; his fifth, a desperately fast one, was short on the leg, and effortlessly lifted over that accursed wall; his last was outside the batsman's reach on the off.

Runs were coming at a terrible pace; and the pace continued, growing faster still, when Gauvinier tried a double change. The hundred went up for no wickets. The wicket-keeper supposed grimly that they'd make about three hundred and declare.

'Oh, you never know your luck!' Gauvinier bravely answered.

'We've got ours. This time.'

Never had the Tillingfold team been seen with tails so lowly drooping or apparently with such good reason. Gauvinier put on his first bowlers again, changing their ends. Marling faced Longman, ran out and drove a good-length ball clean out of the ground—a huge hit. The bowler's face was a study. Marling must have decided where the next ball was going before it was delivered, for he was yards out of his ground to what luckily chanced to be a short long hop; he waved his bat at it, fell forward and was ignominiously stumped.

108—1—89, the score-board read.

A stranger came in, wearing a Sussex Martlet's cap.

'Lord! Look at this!' said Jenkins. 'I'm blowed if we've done with 'em yet.'

But the stranger, deceived no doubt by the queer suddenness of Longman's delivery, played across his first ball and retired with his off stump leaning well back—a very pleasant sight to the Tillingfold team. No more wickets and no more runs that over. Gauvinier bowled a maiden, which was so refreshing after the orgy of runs that the tails of the Tillingfold team visibly rose; but they drooped during Longman's next, which he started with a juicy full toss and followed by a juicier long hop knee-high on the leg side—a gift of eight runs which was quietly taken; then he settled down and the last four balls were a good length.

Gauvinier is as likely to remember the next over as he is likely to remember that disastrous first. Southernhay, the Wilminghurst skipper, who was set, snicked his first ball and the wicket-keeper took a palpable catch, a good one, too, on the leg side. Gauvinier's next ball shaved the new-comer's wicket, and his third, the new-comer being too anxious to emulate the happy Marling, hit the middle peg. Wilminghurst's chief hitter came in next, a familiar figure, obviously resolved to show visitors what the home side could do in the way of hard hitting, but he, too, began too soon, and drove his first ball back to Gauvinier, who jumped to hold a nice catch. His last ball yorked Number Seven.

119—6—0.

Tom Rutherford came up, quivering with excitement.

'One hundred and fifty on this ground means only ninety on ours. Easily. We're not done yet.'

Sam Bird backed him well up. 'That's right!' he slowly declared with immense emphasis. 'And they've not got one hundred and fifty, I may mention.'

'No. Nor will,' declared the wicket-keeper. 'Lord! what a lark to beat 'em with a side like this!'

'We'll make a show, anyhow,' Tom Rutherford remarked quietly, wisely fearful of over-confidence.

'Any of the new crowd bowlers?' he inquired of their umpire.

'Can't say.'

'Man in!'

They sprang to their places—a different side.

Seven runs came from the erratic Longman's first five, then a beauty knocked the off stump clean out of its hole.

A wily old man came in to bat, and, facing Gauvinier after a one to leg, played the last five balls like an ancient book. If only that beggar could keep a length, thought Gauvinier ardently of the solid, unsmiling Longman. But the beggar could not. Came a full toss that went for two byes, a long hop that went for two runs—the two balls would have been a gift of twelve runs to Marling—one that thumped the clumsy batsman on the chest woke him up, perhaps, for he hit the next one for four and the one after for three. One hundred and thirty was up on the score-board.

Gauvinier's unuttered curse was modified by hope at having a go at that batsman and not at the wily old man. 'He'll cow-shot a good-length ball for four and hit across a half-volley.' He itched to have his chance; bet a hundred to one he'd get him. His chance came. He bowled the ball he wanted to—a half-volley slightly slower—round whirled the bat, well across, down went the wicket. Gauvinier purred to himself like a happy cat, or any bowler who has done precisely what he wanted to do, foreseeing the right ball and bowling it. An absurd call ran the wily old man out. Longman knocked the last wicket down with a furious full toss. Tillingfold had one hundred and thirty-nine to make to win, after one hundred had been on the board for no wickets.

'That's about seventy-five on our ground,' Tom Rutherford kept quietly assuring every member of the team in turn. Gauvinier in sad silence pondered on the batting order. There was no doubt about Number One. Ernest Settatree was a good and careful bat, keen all through, and with any luck might stay there. Lord! how he missed old John McLeod and Trine and Dick Fanshawe and Sid Smith. Still, there were the two Carruthers—the wicket-keeper and his young brother Bill—strong as lions, and, when they got going, dangerous: very dangerous when, oh! when, they got going! There was half an hour's play before tea. If four wickets fell . . . hence loathed melancholy!

'Bill,' he cried cheerfully, 'what about first knock?'

Bill blushed and laughed. 'May as well, first as last.'

'Watch the first few, you young fool' said his brother severely, 'and you'll be right as rain.'

'Not 'alf. You bet. Not if it snows ink!' said Bill, too thrilled at the prospect of going out to bat first to talk perfect sense.

'You've only got to pat 'em to get four here,' said Jenkins, beaming encouragement.

'Oh, I'll pat 'em all right!' quoth Bill.

His elder brother vehemently begged him 'not to act silly'— a way with elder brothers—and Bill replied that he was as Gawd made him—or words to that effect—while he nervously buckled on his pads, and asked young Settatree to let him take first over that he might 'get his' as soon as possible; and again elder brother adjured him with savage vehemence 'not to act so damned silly.'

'The young blighter!' Ted Carruthers bitterly remarked as the batsmen walked out to the wicket. 'He'd be a decent bat if he wouldn't act silly.'

'Number Three, Ted; I'm four, Tom Rutherford five, Jenkins six. . . .'

'Our tail ought to wag, I don't think!' began Ted with grim humour. 'Couldn't raise . . .' But he stopped. The first ball was being bowled. Eyes stared tensely, to see Bill lunge feebly at it, not a hit, not a shot, not even a cow-shot. The ball struck the edge of the bat and soared over slip's head. They ran two.

'Steady, Bill!' roared the enraged Ted, and muttered to his neighbours, 'You'd think he'd never held a bat in his hand before, the young turnip!'

Poor Ted, wounded in his family pride, could only groan as Bill met the next ball with the same futile half-hearted lunge, a shot he never indulged in at the nets, but kept exclusively for matches—hit the ball this time and lifted it high and straight and easy into the hands of deep mid-on.

He came in laughing loudly to hide his miserable discomfiture. 'Haven't kept you waiting long, Ted,' he breezily remarked, and then, unable to keep it up, lamented: 'What I needs make that assish scoop for . . .'

'Yes, you wants a good slap behind yer ears,' growled his brother, choosing a batting-glove. Out he strode, chin forward, to maintain the family honour.

Impatience, however, was a family failing, for, much to little brother's glee, Ted viciously lashed at the first ball he received and missed it apparently by feet.

'Look at that now! Look at that! And he tells me not to have a punch!' cried Bill, convulsed.

But Gauvinier and Tom Rutherford were thankful to observe that he was steadier after that first absurdity, and he and Settatree settled down to play good, sound cricket, picking the right one to hit, and hitting it hard and clean. Every ball was watched with excitement; every run cheered.

Thirty-two was on the board when the teams came in for tea.

Settatree, not out twelve; Ted Carruthers, not out fourteen.

Tensity relaxed during tea, which was taken on a long trestle-table under trees outside the pavilion: huge plates of bread and butter, piled slices of plum cake, tea from an enormous urn. Laughter and chat and vigorous munching; gulps of hot tea, cup after cup.

Tillingfold ate heartily, talked gaily; after the disastrous beginning they were making a good fight of it.

Gauvinier, lighting a cigarette, urged the reluctant umpires out into the sun. The tensity of the game was resumed. Both men went on batting like books, taking no risks, running well, hitting the loose ones hard and true. There was every sign of a stand. Forty went up on the board.

And then one cocked up at young Settatree, point fell forward, rolled over, held up the ball, shouting: 'How's that?' Young Settatree looked towards the bowler's umpire, who hesitated, then half-raised a diffident finger; so he appealed to the other umpire, Sam Bird.

'Ah! I couldn't rightly see,' Sam Bird faltered and called out stoutly to the bowler's umpire: 'How was it?'

'Out!' he snapped, looking at no one, and young Settatree had to retire, a very disgruntled man.

47—2—18.

'It hit the ground first, I'll swear,' said young Settatree, almost weeping, to Gauvinier, whom he passed on his way out to bat.

'Rotten luck, anyhow. You were batting better than I've ever seen you bat before.'

'Give it 'em, Skipper, for the Lord's sake!'

43

Gauvinier went out, sincerely hoping that he would, and clearly praying in his own mind that the bowler might not find his blind spot on the leg stump—large and fatal always for his first few balls.

Providence and the bowler were kind, for down came a shortish good-length ball on the off, which went past cover to the boundary, his favourite shot. The next, pitched farther up, he used his reach to drive pleasantly back to mid-off, who was glad to stop it, and retreated a few yards at the bowler's suggestion. Thank goodness he was seeing them! Thank goodness, too, it did not occur to the bowler to put a man at extra-cover.

Up to nine he kept count of his runs, though he had no wish to do so; it was unsettling; made him in a hurry. Quietly he stayed there; not feeling that each ball might be his last; not visualizing horrid mis-hits, silly mistakes that would be his undoing. The score was mounting; they were putting up seventy. Ted Carruthers was batting soundly, hitting the loose ball hard; two fours: ah! there was eighty going up. No disgrace now. It would be fun to put the hundred up. Oh, here was a good one: shortish on the off, again. Full in the centre of the bat. And no extra-cover, he chuckled to himself, watching the ball thump against the wooden pavilion.

The bowler hopefully set mid-off wider and deeper: and forgetting Gauvinier's length and reach, bowled what would have been a good-length ball to a shorter man. The Tillingfold captain stepped out and hit a half-volley straight past where mid-off was standing before his hopeful shifting—a satisfactory drive to watch as it sped over the fast ground to the boundary.

Ninety went up on the score-board, and the fieldsmen looked at the figures with earnest faces. The Tillingfold team, too excited to sit, kept hurrying to the score-box to see the exact score, cheering each run. Every now and then some supporter of the home team would utter a stentorian request to know what Wilminghurst were up to, now.

And the batsmen had that set, unhurried manner that is so depressing to a fielding side.

There came two maidens as the century approached—two maidens which put the field alert on their toes and dug the batsmen in. Why hurry? After the first three balls of the next over, played confidently back, the strain proved too great for the bowler; he sent down his first bad ball for five overs, a full toss which Ted Carruthers swept out of the ground for six, and the hundred went up amid roars of delight. Then a long hop, pulled fiercely against the wall. He must be nearing his fifty. But out he leapt and lashed viciously at the last ball; he might have been bowled, he might have been stumped, he might have been caught, but none of these sad things happened. He made a complete miss: the ball shaved the off stump; the wicket-keeper fumbled it. Ted scrambled back.

'Steady, Ted; steady!' came the shriek of his young brother, timid to death of the family impatience.

Gauvinier took two nice fours in the next over, and then for the first time the idea entered his mind, anxious till that moment merely to make a decent show and avert disgrace, that they were well on the way towards winning the match! Heavens! They must be near one hundred and twenty now—very near. Curse it! He wished he hadn't realized it, and could just have gone steadily batting on. He finished the over, nervous as when he came out to bat: superstitious really.

Ted hit another four. Shouts of joy acclaimed the fact of his fifty. Then he took another dip, oh! a wild one! There was a nasty snick, slip dived forward, tossed up the ball. 127—3—52.

'Well played, Ted!' shouted Gauvinier, with a sinking in the stomach at the thought how long and thin was the tail. Twelve runs—three fours; twelve runs—three fours, beat rhythmically through his brain.

Tom Rutherford walked in, his face set, a trier every inch of him. Good man. But the sun on his glasses; his sight not so good as it was.

A leg-bye. They ran an easy one.

Marling had been put on. Gauvinier, strung up, had hardly noticed the change of bowling, and had not noticed at all the change of field. Came a medium-fast short one on the off—'Here's one of them,' he thought; 'a gift,' and hit it full and strong, to look up as he ran forward, to find it travelling straight into the hands of extra-cover. He stopped dead in surprise to watch the catch, a good one at the pace the ball was travelling, then walked miserably back to the pavilion, cursing his idiocy. Marling frankly rejoiced. 128—4—46. Jenkins took his place. Marling sent him down a fast yorker on the leg stump, which the ball shaved. The wicket-keeper side-stepped too late, kicked it: two runs. Jenkins waved his bat at the next ball and was bowled. 130—5—0. Oh, Lord! To be so near! Well, anyhow it was a damned good game.

'Fancy being such a fool as to beat it straight into his hands!' Gauvinier spoke to Heaven.

Longman was walking in. He had one shot and one only. A little half-step forward, a mighty circular lurch to leg: a good-length ball on the middle or leg stump hit the bat and went for four. At everything else he pushed his bat daintily sideways, slowly and cunningly and always ineffectually.

Marling was taking no risks. He bowled a good-length ball on the leg stump—right on to the swinging bat, and, with astonishment, saw it go for four. Gauvinier began to laugh, almost hysterical with amusement and the game's thrill. Wild cheers rent the air. Another good-length ball hit the lurching bat, but not quite full this time, so that it missed the fieldsman, brought up after the last shot. He saved the four, though; and they ran two. Only three more! Only three more! But shortish ones on the off followed, at which Longman dabbed warily, and, luckily, failed to touch.

The first ball of the next over beat Tom Rutherford all ends up and passed not more than one inch over the bails. At the second, anxious to make sure of the game, he lunged gallantly out, hit, skied, and was caught and bowled.

136—6.

Followed the boy, and all the fieldsmen crowded cruelly near. But all four balls he gamely managed to stop.

'Will he now, oh, will he bowl on his bat?' Gauvinier ached to think, watching, with horror, Marling place another man on the leg side.

It is difficult for any bowler to realize that a man can have one shot and one only like a mechanical toy. Down came the good-length ball on the middle stump—hit the swinging bat, flew between the fieldsmen—struck the wall.

Too late Marling realized his mistake. He sent a slow, high

full toss, an absolutely fatal ball to Longman, who tried to pat it with his bat as with a tennis racket, and was bowled.

But the impossible had happened. Tillingfold with eight men and a boy had beaten Wilminghurst, after a hundred had stood on the score-board, for the first time in the annals of Tillingfold cricket, for no wickets.

HOW OUR VILLAGE BEAT
THE AUSTRALIANS

(To Arthur Somerset)

HERE they were—these great Australians with their unbeaten record—to speak to any of whom by chance even or mistake, in a railway carriage, would have been an unforgettable honour; here they actually were in full strength dressed and ready to play us, stepping about on our own ground—cracking jokes like ordinary men. No wonder our hearts beat, our eyes bulged, our knees weakened, for after all it is one thing to talk of having a go at the Australians and quite another to see them in flesh and blood before you. The thing seemed barely credible. Sam Bird, who always likes to be careful in his statements—never anxious, you understand, to commit himself in any way—said to me as I stood quailing:

'On the whole they're a pretty decent side, I should say; perhaps the strongest side that has ever appeared on a village ground.'

'Ah, well, on paper!'—I answered, my natural optimism asserting itself immediately. 'And there is always the luck of the game to be taken into account.'

'True for you,' Sam slowly laughed. 'You never know your luck!'

One kept blinking to make quite sure that one's eyes were not playing tricks: but they were not. They were recording plain facts as faithfully as human eyes ever can—which persist, however, in affirming the monotonous rigidity of the earth, against our certain knowledge that it is rushing round the sun in space.

There stood Mr. Armstrong, a little larger even than life, tossing with our Captain. Mr. Armstrong, as always, tossed with great skill, and showed no surprise at winning. He elected to bat without a moment's hesitation, not pausing for a moment to consider the old familiar argument that it is a good thing to know what you have to make before going in to make them. He showed no nervousness of any kind: indeed it was desolating for us to observe the complete confidence that marked the deportment of our visitors. Some of us were cowardly enough to wish that we had left the Australians unchallenged. There was a look too of amusement on the faces of the spectators, who were crowding upon the ground, as though they had left their homes not so much to watch a game of cricket as to see some fun.

Jovial remarks were flung out to us from the safety of the crowded ring—to keep our tails up—to show what we were made of—to remember that no game was lost till it was won. I regret to say they were on the facetious rather than on the encouraging side.

Mr. Collins and Mr. Gregory opened the batting to the bowling of Sid Smith and Mr. Gauvinier. Our side was fairly strong, the same indeed, with two exceptions, as that which defeated Raveley. On paper our side did not look much perhaps; on the field, however, there were great possibilities about it.

Sam Bird, asked to give centre to Mr. Collins, could hardly speak or move; but eventually Mr. Collins obtained as good a block as he has ever obtained in a Test Match.

The curious happenings, which I shall accurately relate as my eyes beheld them, began immediately. For Sid Smith, bewildered by the occasion, bowled as soon as Sam Bird stood back and a little too soon for Mr. Collins, who was not quite ready. Had this occurred in a Test Match, Mr. Collins would undoubtedly have stepped away declining to play the ball, but in this game, as the ball was a full toss, Mr. Collins perhaps opined that he was ready enough to place it out of the ground: for this he gallantly tried to do, but unfortunately he missed the ball altogether and it hit his middle stump.

He looked pardonably and intensely annoyed; Sid and Paul Gauvinier, both real sportsmen, instantly ran up, Sid apologizing and Mr. Gauvinier pointing out that the umpire had omitted to cry 'Play!' (which was true: Sam Bird's lips had indeed moved, but no audible sound had emerged from them). Mr. Gauvinier begged Mr. Collins to remain where he was, not wishing to take an unfair advantage of any visiting team; in the interests of the game he begged him to stay, and Mr. Collins very obligingly consented to do so. The ball was considered as a no ball, as though it had never been bowled;

and the game was resumed, or perhaps it would be more accurate to say, properly begun.

Sam Bird found his voice and bravely shouted 'Play!' and we all got ready on our toes, taking heart at the mere sight of an Australian wicket broken, however the breaking may have been caused.

Now I am a trained observer and was in a position to see what happened next. Sid bowled his usual medium-to-slow-paced ball on the off stump, and it was a perfect length. Mr. Collins played well forward—to drive it, firmly but not hard, past mid-off: but the ball, instead of striking the bat, rose, as though bouncing on some invisible substance or lifted by some unseen spirit hand, and, describing a neat half-circle over the shoulder of his bat, hit the centre of the off stump.

There was a hush of surprise, then a roar of applause. Mr. Collins looked at his bat and looked at the wicket and looked at the pitch. Mr. Collins looked scared. He stooped to pick up the ball; he pinched it, he smelt it, as though in doubt of its being a cricket ball at all; then he uttered a deep-felt ejaculation of regret and withdrew towards our pavilion. He will worry about that ball as long as he worries about anything, and how it came to bowl him. But it was all over, as these tragic and mysterious things always are, in a tiny fraction of a second, and no one exists who can really enlighten us as to their exact nature. Even if we happen to be told the truth, we are not able to believe it. We are in fact the merest Horatios and there is far, far more in heaven and earth and also on the cricket field than is dreamed of in our philosophies.

o—1—o, the score-board read; a familiar, and I may add, under the circumstances, a refreshing sight. Our Secretary, Mr. John McLeod, walked up to Sid Smith, and told him that it was the finest ball he had ever seen bowled. Sid blushed and believed him and hoped that a member of the English Selection Committee was on the ground, and making a note of his name.

Mr. Armstrong came in next, slow, massive and imperturbable, his enormous belief in his side and himself towering above the little wanton vagaries of Chance.

'Not a bad ball *that*, I should say!' he remarked cheerfully to Sid, twiddling his bat round in his hand, making it look a funny little instrument for such a great man to be using.

Still thrilled by what my eyes had beheld, I rather hoped that nothing unforeseen would happen to him. Moreover, o—2—o on the score-board would really be past a joke, would indeed appear almost blasphemous treatment of our august visitors. The Australian Captain was the Australian Captain, and *lèse majesté* is not an empty formula to any but a Communist heart. Perhaps some such thoughts moved Sid, for much to my relief his next ball was a half-volley outside the leg stump which Mr. Armstrong swept gracefully clean out of the ground, narrowly missing a motor that was passing along in the road, its occupants oblivious of who were playing in our field: thus many golden opportunities are missed, as we rush along our modern way at an ever faster pace. Eager small boys found and returned the ball, hopeful of much similar work: but Mr. Armstrong, though his confidence towered above Chance, yet took no liberties with that fickle lady; and played the remaining four balls of the over as any decent first-wicket batsman would have played four good-length balls in his first over.

Tillingfold crossed over, and Mr. Gauvinier started to bowl to Mr. Gregory, and it was clear that Mr. Gregory had the length of the game well in mind, and was determined to waste no time, for the first ball he slashed confidently past cover with such force that it overcame the longish grass and reached the boundary. Two ones followed, confident hard drives which young Mr. Trine flung back from the deep. Mr. Armstrong was backing up with a little more exuberance perhaps than he would have done in a Test Match, suggesting a readiness to play the excellent game of tip-and-run; Mr. Gauvinier bowled a good-length ball on the off stump: Mr. Gregory stepped out and drove it straight back with tremendous force to the bowler, whose hand the ball viciously smacked and then struck the wicket. Unfortunately Mr. Armstrong was a good yard outside his crease and his own umpire was obliged to give him out in response to the yell of appeal that came simultaneously from point, slip, and Mr. Gauvinier, and was taken up immediately from sheer joyous excitement by most of our remaining fieldsmen.

Mr. Armstrong reluctantly withdrew, an illustrious victim of misfortune, and all of us within earshot condoled with him, sincerely, crying out, 'Oh, bad luck, sir, bad luck!'

He smiled and remarked without a quaver in his voice, like the great sportsman that he is: 'It's all in the game, boys; it's all in the game.'

Somehow, we most of us felt guilty, and longed to put him back again at the wicket; but it could not of course be done. Even a great Australian Captain must bow before his fate and the rules of the game.

Mr. Ryder strode in to join Mr. Gregory, and caused considerable amusement to the spectators by hastening to take centre before he realized that he was not to receive the bowling.

Sam Bird started to run from square-leg to the wicket, confident that he and not the famous batsman must be at fault.

He paused half-way and looked wildly round, before returning to his place with his accustomed composure.

Not in the least daunted by the bad start, Mr. Ryder and Mr. Gregory played good free cricket, and it seemed probable that they might make a stand, as the bowling neither of Sid Smith nor of Mr. Gauvinier appeared to trouble them greatly. Twenty was on the score-board; and though Mr. Armstrong and Mr. Collins were out—two useful men to see the back of in any match—signs of uneasiness began to be shown among the Tillingfold team.

Mr. Gregory was lashing good-length balls a little outside the off stump between point and cover; Teddy White was fielding cover and retreated to the boundary by the hedge. Our Secretary, Mr. John McLeod, fearless and short and stout (fearless, that is, of anything but the possible effect of a sudden stoop), was fielding point and came squarer, though the balls seemed generally to have passed him before he was quite aware that they had been hit. He was unaccustomed to the shot and to its pace. Once or twice he had fallen over in a frantic but tardy effort to reach the ball. This had called forth little shouts of laughter from the happy spectators who were not fielding point to Mr. Gregory, and old John McLeod felt that he was somehow being made game of, for a smile was noticeable even upon the courteous face of Mr. Gregory.

I watched this little side-show, as it were, with increasing interest, full of that strained ominous sensation, familiar to us all in dreams, that something startling was about to happen.

Mr. Gregory, with those steel-strong wrists of his, lashed

at the ball and hit it a beautiful smack: and I saw Mr. McLeod bounce yards to the right with his arm extended, and his arm seemed to stretch out like a piece of elastic; there was another smack, following the first quickly as two reports from a gun. Mr. McLeod spun completely round and sat quietly down with a dazed look upon his face, holding up the caught ball in his right hand, between his fingers and thumb.

Mr. Gregory had started running, thinking his hit was safely away to Teddy White—the howls and yells of joy at the catch stopped him. He stared at Mr. McLeod, bewildered.

'I caught it all right,' our Secretary faltered, and began slowly to rise from his sitting posture. 'It stuck, you know.'

Mr. Gregory continued to stare, first at Mr. McLeod, then out towards Teddie White, in the direction he was sure the ball had travelled, half suspecting, I believe, that Mr. McLeod had played a trick upon him and produced another ball, like a conjurer, from the slack of his breeches.

But Mr. Gregory, though a little dazed with astonishment, was clear-minded enough to perceive that there was no slack to Mr. McLeod's breeches or, indeed, to any other part of his attire, which fitted him like a glove. The Australian umpire answered his questioning look with becoming promptness:

'Out!' he called, and added to Mr. Gauvinier: 'The most wonderful catch I have ever seen.'

Our Secretary quickly recovered from his momentary surprise as we crowded round him, asking him however he had managed to bring it off. He was so happy that he was on the brink of tears. 'The sort of catch I've often dreamed of making,' he stammered. 'And now I've done it, bless my soul! Now I've done it; and in this game too!'

'We are all inspired once in our lives,' said young Trine, who had come hurrying up from the deep.

'Inspired! Ah, that's the very word,' gasped old John, more breathless than usual. 'Do you know I was that mad to catch it, I felt lifted up and shoved towards it, and as though my arm had got stretched out three times its natural length at least.'

'That's exactly what it looked like, mate,' said Sid Smith in solemn tones. And to the world at large he added: 'This is what comes of playing cricket on a Sunday!' a remark which it baffled me to understand, though local people are often superstitious. Old John McLeod, I thought, looked hurt. But the happy cluster round our honest Secretary broke up as Mr. Andrews strode to the wicket, and the catch, like other great events in human existence, became a thing of the past; a thing to be recounted to grandchildren by every person who had seen it; a thing of history; a thing, moreover, so rarely wonderful in itself that it could not possibly be embellished in the telling.

24—3—11. Tillingfold were not doing so badly. It was clear that they were no longer content to make an exhibition of themselves for the country's sake; they were all out now to make a game of it; forgetting in their enthusiasm and excitement that any batsman on the other side might be considered good enough for at least a hundred. If fat old John McLeod could at a pinch hold a catch like that, hang it all! why shouldn't anyone? Thus ran the tenor of their thought.

'Does he often do that?' Mr. Andrews asked our stumper pleasantly, as he made his block, smiling.

'Oh, well! Not very often, now,' our stumper bashfully replied.

Sid Smith was now bowling with more than his usual unconcern, as though he were at length convinced that he could but do his best and that the outcome of his effort lay in other hands than his. There was something impersonal and aloof about his attitude, and his attitude was perhaps a wise one under the circumstances, though in an ordinary game it might have robbed his bowling of sting and intention. But this, it will be noted, was not an ordinary game.

Of course in cricket, the game being played with a moving ball (sometimes a very swiftly moving ball), things happen so quickly and are over so soon that no one can be quite sure precisely what did happen to any given ball. Thus it is we hear even from experts such divergent accounts of the same stroke. The game, indeed, is wrapped in a cloud of mystery which can never be pierced. Herein lies its fascination. The player feels himself in touch with some hidden power, when, for example, leaping out to his full length the bowler takes and holds a flying ball he can barely see. It is not done by taking thought. The man who has ever held a hot return from his own bowling feels that it has somehow been done for him, and feels grateful; the man who has unaccountably missed a sitter at mid-off, which ninety-nine times out of a hundred he would have held, feels that he has been the victim of a spiteful trick.

On the cricket field we are in touch with powers to which, though we may not be in a position to name and label them, as in this mechanical age we like to name and label everything, it is as well to be respectful. It was natural that in such a game as this these powers should be in special evidence, and it was natural that such a simple, unsophisticated soul as Sid Smith should be specially open to their influence. There was something comic, no doubt, in the dogged perseverance of his bowling, but there was also something very touching in its faithfulness and simplicity.

Now some of us read with surprise that Jack Hobbs, after playing the Australian bowling for a whole day, was bowled on the opening of the second day by a full toss from Mr. Mailey. We had learned at our preparatory schools that a full toss was a good ball to smite. Jack Hobbs himself, however, in the interesting account of the tour which he contributed to a daily newspaper, described himself as being quite content to be out to such a ball, which, we are told, was deceptive in pace, swerved in its flight, hung in the air, and beat him all ends up before bowling him.

I must own to having been sceptical about this until with my own eyes I saw the ball with which Sid Smith disturbed the wicket of Mr. Ryder. It, too, was a full toss, a slow full toss, which I thought, and Mr. Ryder obviously thought, must reach him knee-high, wide of the wicket on the leg side. But, half-way in its flight, just after Mr. Ryder had turned, his mind, in that fraction of a second during which a batsman unconsciously decides to act, made up, his strength summoned half-way in its flight, I say, the ball miraculously seemed to pause and swerve inwards. Mr. Ryder, observing this, made a superb effort to change his mind, only possible to such a fine batsman as he is, but in spite of his almost superhuman quickness of eye and wrist, he was too late; he overbalanced as the ball swerved gently past him and on to the middle stump and neatly saved himself from a fall by the help of his bat. A clumsier man would certainly have fallen.

Mr. Macartney came in next, looking perceptibly worried

at the way things were going. A village wicket might be accountable for a great deal, but no wicket could be blamed for disaster caused by a full toss.

There was a business-like look about him, the air of one who without being the least downhearted or inclined to sit upon the splice, was yet determined to take no foolish risks. It was evident that he considered the previous batsmen had been victims either of gross ill-luck, like Mr. Armstrong, or of their own folly.

Three runs were made without any untoward incident. Mr. Macartney and his partner seemed to be wondering how four good wickets could have fallen; their voices as they called, to run or not to run, had that settled confidence of men who are ready to go quietly on till their Captain sees fit to declare. But this was not to be.

Mr. Macartney drove Mr. Gauvinier past mid-off into the deep to young Mr. Trine. As the batsmen passed, Mr. Andrews said, 'There's another,' and there seemed no doubt whatever that there was ample time for a second run.

Mr. Trine was fielding alertly and well—he saw their intention to take a second run: at full speed he picked the ball up and flung it in with such force and accuracy that the middle stump was knocked clean out of the ground. It was fortunate the stump was not broken, as there might have been considerable difficulty in obtaining another: and we never like to ask any side to finish the game with incomplete kit. Mr. Andrews, noticing the amazing velocity of the throw, quickened his pace, but being a good yard outside the crease was forced to retire.

You could not call the piece of work that dismissed him with any justice a fluke. True, Mr. Trine did not usually throw with such pace and accuracy: indeed, he seemed spirited to the ball even as the ball was spirited to the wicket; but most men rise to an occasion once at least in their lives; and that was the occasion on which Mr. Trine rose; nor could he have chosen a better. It is unlikely that he will ever forget that piece of fielding; it is certain that he will never repeat it.

Tillingfold continued to do quite nicely; five wickets were now down for thirty-three. Of course, the Australian tail might wag, though tails rarely did on our own ground, for long.

Now our Captain, Mr. Gauvinier, is always made to win; some people say that he over-anxious, too keen. He may possibly be; but I think he was wise to remind the side that they had to face some pretty decent bowling. He did not over-do it, as he would have done had he gone on to remind us that on several well-authenticated occasions all ten wickets of a side had fallen without a run being scored. We had all read these lamentable records at the end of Mr. Somerset's score-book; and they had long been present somewhere at the back of most of our minds as a painful possibility, though no one, I am glad to say, had had the indecency to put the horrid thought into words.

Mr. Mailey came in quite unabashed by the figures on the score-board. By the way he took centre you felt he was going to make things hum. He did. He leaped out at Mr. Gauvi-nier's first ball and hit it full and tremendously hard. I thought it must have gone well into the next field. I was astonished accordingly to hear Mr. Gauvinier call out, in a loud com-manding voice, 'Mine!' I looked up, and there the ball was soaring higher and higher; so high indeed that Mr. Mailey and Mr. Macartney easily ran two before the ball descended into Mr. Gauvinier's safe hands, about a yard and a half be-hind the umpire. The way in which Mr. Gauvinier avoided treading on the wicket was extremely clever.

Tillingfold have always been proud of their fielding. They had certainly never shown to better advantage. 'The feller deserves to be out,' growled Mr. Macartney, 'swiping at his first ball in that silly fashion.'

Mr. Mailey walked jauntily out, laughing to himself, pre-tending bravely, as many another good cricketer has pre-tended on that sad walk to the pavilion after failing to score, that after all it didn't so very much matter.

Small boys were pacing up and down before the pavilion peering in to catch a glimpse of Mr. Armstrong's face; but the features of such a man are under perfect control, and they learned nothing of what was passing behind the cheerful mask within the great man's mind. All captains should strive to acquire this imperturbability of feature, as a rattled skipper is apt to mean a disjointed side. Mr. Armstrong's bearing was indeed a lesson to us all. His plan had no doubt been to make a couple of hundred or so for the loss of one or perhaps two wickets, to take tea and then skittle us twice out for twenty or perhaps thirty. But the gods who preside over cricket had decided otherwise; the unforeseen had happened; and six good wickets were down for thirty-three. Nothing can alter a fact of this kind: each fallen wicket helped to form, like boulders, a horrid little cairn of incontrovertible fact.

The remaining Australian batsmen gave us little trouble, and nobody expected that they would. As Sid Smith wisely remarked: 'We had 'em on the run,' and a side in that condition, as everyone knows, can do nothing right. Our men, on the other hand, did nothing whatever wrong. Every semblance of a catch was held, and some, indeed, that hardly bore any ordinary resemblance to a catch. That, for instance, with which young Mr. Trine dismissed Mr. McDonald was quite miraculous. The ball, travelling at the deadly breast-high level of a furious drive, seemed well out of reach; but Mr. Trine, speeding over the rough ground with the effortless ease of a man moving like a porpoise through water in his dreams, did reach it and he held it superbly in his outstretched hand. Wonderful as the catch was, he never looked like missing it.

The Australian innings closed at thirty-nine—a trebly unlucky number.

There was time for thirty-five minutes' batting before the tea interval at five. It created a very favourable impression that quite a number of the Australian team walked with a hand on the roller, while we rolled the wicket.

Some of us were wondering whether Mr. Armstrong, in view of important matches that were to be played during the week, would think it wiser to rest his fast bowlers, in spite of the fact that the wicket would certainly suit them; and distrustful eyes were turned on certain unobtrusive plantains that, do what we would, continued to disfigure the square.

As the roller was shoved up by the hedge I noticed an Eastern gentleman who was staying in the village and was rumoured to be a Tibetan monk of very high grade, left standing alone. He approached each wicket and inspected the stumps, stroking each one gently between his finger and thumb, as though to find out the quality of the material of which they were made. Sam Bird told me that, before the game began, he had asked to be allowed to handle the ball, and Sam had allowed him to do so.

'Ah, how ingenious men are!' he had remarked, as he politely handed the ball back to Sam.

Sam Bird likes to do everything properly. He realized that our visitors were accustomed to play on county grounds where a bell is rung to warn spectators off the ground and to prepare the team for taking the field. There is no bell on our ground; the umpires stroll out and we follow at our leisure; so thoughtful Sam, afraid that the Australians might be put off their game by the absence of the tintinnabulation to which their ears were accustomed, had brought a small bell, and this he produced from his trouser pocket and shook violently for some moments, standing discreetly, being a shy man, behind the small scoring-box. Then, with some difficulty replacing the bell in his trouser pocket, he joined his colleague and proceeded with a solemn shy smile upon his broad face to the wicket, followed by the Australian team in a laughing, compact body.

Our Secretary, dear old John McLeod, who was going in first and always took first ball, turned a little pale when he saw that Mr. Armstrong, suitably impressed by Tillingfold's magnificent fielding, was setting his field for a fast bowler.

'Oh dear!' he said. 'Bless my soul, now. Oh, well. One ball. How I should dearly love to play a ball or two.'

'You just stop there till tea,' said Mr. Gauvinier pleasantly, patting him on the back. 'And we shall be all right.'

'It's no good waiting,' said Mr. Bois, a preparatory schoolmaster who lived in the village and had played much really good cricket. 'Come on. The sound old rules hold good, you know. Keep your eye on the ball and use a nice straight bat.'

They made their brave way to the wicket.

Dear old John McLeod must have felt not more than about three inches high, as all alone he faced Mr. McDonald and the ten Australian fieldsmen, placed by a master mind on the exact spot towards which, if he did happen to strike the ball, the ball must certainly fly. Mr. McDonald came thundering along his terrific run to the wicket, a giant with a cannon ball which a man feeling like a midget was to receive with a bat that felt like half a wax match in the midget's grasp. The odds were disproportionate. But our Secretary, all honour to him, gripped the handle of his bat, glued his eye on something he took to be the ball and played the ball.

Its impact on the centre of his bat gave Mr. McLeod such confidence that he grew from a mere midget of a few inches to almost half his full stature as a man. True, he dwindled a little as Mr. McDonald walked leisurely into the outfield preparatory to delivering his next ball, but during the course of the five seconds' sprint to the wicket he had time to grow once more, and once more the ball met the bat, though sooner than Mr. McLeod had expected. This second stroke drew a round of applause from the spectators, confident now that the batsman had taken the measure of the bowling. The next ball, however, missed the bat. Mr. Oldfield, confident that it must hit the wicket, missed it also and it sped to the boundary for four runs.

Thus Tillingfold's worst fears of dismissal without scoring were allayed. A jubilant smile spread slowly over many of the faces of the team in the pavilion.

'Oh Lord,' Horace Cairie muttered, 'if we could only beat them!' And he kept doing the sum six sixes are thirty-six in his mind, and wishing it were possible that a bye or a leg-bye could sometimes score six.

The next ball also missed the bat, and missed the wicket. I was standing straight behind the stumps and I was as surprised as Mr. Oldfield and Mr. McDonald at Mr. McLeod's escape. I could have sworn that the top of the wicket faded for that fraction of a second when the ball should have struck it. But there stood the wicket, bails on, unbroken. Mr. Oldfield walked up to the stumps, put both his gloved hands on them, and pressed them, as wicket-keepers sometimes do, backwards and forwards, as though to assure himself that there was no deception.

Mr. McDonald may be pardoned for stamping with vexation when the same thing happened to all the remaining balls of his over except the last, which Mr. McLeod steered with a quick flick of his wrist through a small crowd of slips bang against the pavilion for four.

I did not know that Mr. McLeod kept such a shot in his locker. But it has been well said that good bowling evokes latent powers from a batsman. Mr. Bois was never tired of impressing this upon us when urging us, as he frequently did, to make a point of playing better sides. It was chiefly through his advocacy, as the son of a millionaire who had great influence in Melbourne attended his school, that the game had been arranged.

Mr. Bois played with his usual unruffled composure, though his wicket too was often missed by a miracle. Once the wicket was perceptibly hit and perceptibly trembled, but the bails remained stolidly in their place; and there was nothing wrong with the set of the wicket or with the bails, because Mr. Oldfield tapped the stumps lightly with his finger and the bails dropped lightly off. Their umpire, too, came forward and shook the wicket as Mr. Oldfield had done.

It must have been thankless work for their bowlers, for I suppose our first-wicket batsmen might perhaps be considered mere rabbits to bowlers of their class, and to keep shaving the stumps of a rabbit is distressing to any bowler. Then these men, it must be remembered, had the honour of a great Commonwealth to sustain; and to them therefore these elusive wickets must have been doubly, nay, trebly trying. They clutched their heads, they stamped their feet, they jerked their arms down as though punching imaginary heads: and ever the confidence of the two batsmen became more bland and smiling, as well it may have done. The way the Australian bowlers stuck to their thankless task commanded our admiration and roused our unstinted applause.

Runs, however, did not come so fast as in the first over. Mr. Oldfield was alert behind the stumps; the small crowd of slips were on their toes: the fielding, though not miraculous, was very good. Ten, however, crept up on the board, and our batsmen would certainly have remained together until the tea interval, had not Mr. Bois, in playing back to Mr. Mc-Donald, unfortunately struck his wicket with his bat. The one blemish to his style is that he is apt to cramp his freedom of movement by making his block unnecessarily far back from the front crease.

11—1—5 the score-board read, and though Tillingfold as a team would have liked to have knocked off the thirty-nine runs without loss, the start could not be described as other than quite satisfactory. Mr. Bois, however, was extremely annoyed. He was quite at home, he said, and could have stayed there for hours, had it not been for his execrable luck.

Young Mr. Trine, who came in next, noticing that Mr. Old-field was standing well back and that there was no fieldsman in the deep, determined to have a go. As Mr. McDonald was taking his sprint to the wicket he shambled along out of his ground to meet him and letting madly fly, drove him well out of the ground. A few small boys remained husky for the remainder of the day after the prolonged yell which the fine daring of this hit elicited.

He tried to repeat this manœuvre on the last ball of the over, but he started too soon and got too far out of his ground, so that Mr. McDonald and Mr. Oldfield foresaw his intention and acting like one man, Mr. McDonald bowled a slow high full toss over Mr. Trine's head into the hands of Mr. Oldfield, who, still on the run, stumped him—a brilliant piece of concerted work between bowler and wicket-keeper.

'Ah!' said Sid Smith sagely, wagging his head. 'You dussn't take no liberties with such as they.'

During tea, as is usually the case, the strain of the contest was relaxed. The Tillingfold team, especially those who had not yet faced the fast bowlers, seemed to enjoy the honour of eating with their distinguished visitors even more than the honour of playing cricket with them.

Crowds paraded in front of the pavilion, glancing in, as to many it was quite as thrilling to know how the Australians drank their tea and ate their cake and bread and butter as to watch them bat and bowl. Our visitors showed no surprise at this interest, since the trait is common to the inhabitants of both continents, and were no more put off their food by spectators than they were put off their game by them.

Many of the Tillingfold team, however, unused to the glare of publicity, were painfully affected and, much to the distress of their thoughtful captain, ate and drank next to nothing—comparatively speaking—though the caterer had provided a special tea and had raised the price from ninepence to one shilling.

Punctual to the moment Sam Bird, a cake in his mouth, a pastry in his hand (sensible fellow, his bashfulness had limits) tore himself from the table and producing the little bell from his trouser pocket, rang it vigorously, faithful to duty and unheeding the rude remarks of small boys who gathered eagerly about him as he leaned against the small scoring-box.

The umpires went out together. Mr. Armstrong led his men once more into the field, with a look at the score-board, which read 17—2—6. The great game was resumed, Mr. Fanshawe joining our Secretary at the wicket.

Mr. Fanshawe takes his cricket very seriously. He is a religious bat, treating a half-volley or a long hop on the leg with reverence. He was in fact the ideal man to bat first in a Test Match where time is no consideration: during the first week he would have played himself steadily in, and towards the end of the second week he would have begun to make runs, and no one knows how freely he might not have scored as the innings proceeded. But in the Tillingfold games, having always felt hurried, he had never really done himself justice—a born Test Match player in village cricket: another square peg in a round hole. Alas! Life abounds with them.

No doubt Mr. McDonald and Mr. Gregory hoped that, after being refreshed with a cup of tea and a bite of bread and butter, they would be able to hit the wickets; but though they bowled uncommonly well and frequently beat the batsmen the wickets remained intact, as they had done before tea.

In the first half-hour two leg-byes were scored off their bowling; and Mr. Armstrong, feeling that his fast bowlers were expensive and fatiguing themselves to no good purpose, made a double change, going on himself with Mr. Mailey.

Mr. McLeod, never a forcing bat, became infected with Mr. Fanshawe's religious caution, and the atmosphere was so charged with reverence that a run off the bat began to appear like a profanity.

The crowd, at first respectful at the steady resistance to the Australian attack, at last grew restive and disrespectful. Indeed they showed signs of barracking, thinking possibly that it was a mistake to be playing for a draw with twenty-one runs to make to win and more than an hour's time to make them in. They barracked to deaf ears: Mr. McLeod and Mr. Fanshawe, even had their tenacity of purpose allowed them to hear a sound, were not light-natured enough to be distracted by popular opinion, much as each loved his fellow man off the cricket ground. Mr. Mailey tried every conceivable wile to tempt Mr. Fanshawe to hit; but Mr. Fanshawe was not to be tempted. Around both batsmen all the fieldsmen clustered in indescribable positions, sillier than silly. But both batsmen were well content to smother every ball that might under ordinary circumstances have hit the wicket, and let all others severely alone. In the second half-hour after tea, one more leg-bye had been scored. Twenty stood on the score-board—it looked with a quarter of an hour to go as though the match must end in a draw.

Big cricket is a game of infinite uncertainty. At last, in desperation, Mr. Andrews, unable to bear it any longer, literally flung himself at Mr. Fanshawe's bat just as the ball struck it, and caught him well within the crease. It looked more like a tackle at Rugby football than a catch at cricket; and Mr. Fanshawe, rather bewildered, appealed against it, but he appealed in vain. The catch was unusual and unorthodox, but he was indubitably out.

Teddie White came in next. Australians or no Australians he came in, as he always came in, at a half-trot, shouldering his bat, to get to business with as little delay as possible. He disliked formalities, leaving them gladly to what he called 'the rank and stink.'

Mr. Armstrong, caught no doubt after this slow hour in the general assumption that runs were a profanity, or perhaps thinking that the Tillingfold captain had given his men instructions to play for a draw, neglected to replace his field: they were only a little less on the cluster round Teddie White than they had been round Mr. Fanshawe.

Teddie White did not go in for niceties; he didn't bother about the field; it didn't matter to him where they happened to be placed; his one aim in batting was to put the ball out of their reach, out of the ground, much the safest place. But he had a kind heart, and noticing that the fieldsmen were crowded rather nearer to him than they usually were, as Mr. Armstrong bowled, he cried out: 'Look out for yourselves then,' as he might have done to careless boys at the village net, and lashed it for four.

There was a roar of applause. But Teddie White was not pleased. It was an ass of a shot—all along the ground—he had not properly got hold of it at all—you could never hit a six like that, the only really safe shot.

Mr. Armstrong much dislikes to be caught napping. He

set his master mind to work, sized up his man exactly with one piercing look, and proceeded to dot his men carefully along the leg-side boundary, confident that the next ball would prove this reckless hitter's downfall.

Teddie chafed at the delay, muttering to himself: 'If I be dratted fool enough not to beat it over their Aussie 'eads!'

At length, Mr. Armstrong, satisfied with the exact position of his field, swung in his next delivery with a quiet smile of confidence. Teddie White burst at it in mad fury like an explosion; not a muscle, not a nerve in his body but he used for that frenzied blow—the vein on his forehead even bulged, as he smote the ball whizzing over the pavilion.

'That's one on 'em!' he muttered, crumpling off his little cap and rubbing his thick neck with it. 'Two more of 'em and we wins—with a few to spare.'

Just as some writers, charming gentle fellows to meet, can only become vocal when they are in a thoroughly bad temper with life, so Teddie White could only do himself full justice as a batsman in a mood of concentrated fury, as though it were an outrage that eleven men should band themselves together to do him out of a knock—especially when he never failed to pay his subscription to the club.

The delay in collecting the ball added to his exasperation. Like some sort of inspired fiend he crashed at Mr. Armstrong's next delivery and whanged it over the hedge, over the road and into the garden of a house opposite the ground.

The excitement became delirious. Everyone stood up and shouted and yelled and cheered: men waved their hats, and flung them towards the sky: women waved their scarves and handkerchiefs.

'That's another of 'em,' Teddie White muttered, giving his face and neck another vindictive rub with his little cap.

'Well hit, sir, well hit!' said Mr. Armstrong, the sportsman in him never wavering at the most critical moment of any game.

Teddie White glared. He was not to be conciliated by any honeyed words. He growled to himself, 'Well 'it! I'll show the blokes well 'it.' But his fury was part of his batting rather than of his nature, and he looked very red and very shy and very happy.

There was a hush in the roaring, a stillness among the fluttering, waving apparel, one of those tense moments that last a lifetime as Mr. Armstrong delivered the last ball of his over. Spectators held their breath and stared: the only sound was the puff-puff of a belated traction engine as it slowly passed the ground. No one noticed anything funny in the way Teddie White's little crumpled cap sat balanced upon his square head.

For once in his life Mr. Armstrong was rattled and did not bowl the ball he intended to bowl; the intended half-volley across which Teddie would certainly have hit became a full toss, at which Teddie viciously slashed with all his furious strength; the ball soared a terrific height, higher and higher; the outfielders hopefully watched it, retreating towards the hedge. Then, as the clamour of joy rose, it began to fall and fell straight down the smoke-vomiting chimney of the be-lated traction engine.

But what is this that is happening? Mr. Oldfield excitedly appealing! The Australians flocking round the wicket! Could the game not be ours now after such a hit? We were all in consternation—having kept our eyes fixed on the ball. But Teddie in the fury of his last blow had managed to jolt off his little crumpled cap which had impishly floated on to the wicket and now sat perched there even more comfortably than it had before perched on his own square head.

It appears that Teddie, feeling an instant draught on his bald head, had started to snatch his cap from the stumps. To the eternal honour of the Australians they had persuaded him from this rash act, for had he dislodged the bail in removing his cap before the ball had safely landed down the traction engine's chimney he would of course have been out. As it was, he was still in . . .

The whole ground rose and flew at him, the air was thick with fluttering scarves, roaring men, yelling boys, waving arms; even the pavilion rose and streamed like a pennon through the air. The Downs themselves swelled to moun-tains—the houses capered like lambs, as we carried Teddie White, chanting songs of triumph, through the village High Street.

*

And I awoke, alone on the Tillingfold Cricket Ground, with a few toddlers playing about, that lovely Sunday after-noon; and walked smiling home to tea.

HOW OUR VILLAGE TRIED TO PLAY THE AUSTRALIANS

No one knows or will ever know now how the secret leaked out, and turned what was to be essentially an informal and friendly affair into an event of national, nay, world-wide importance. It was natural enough that the present Australian team should wish to have a go at the village which had been audacious enough even to dream of beating Mr. Armstrong's victorious eleven; and the match had been arranged on the understanding that they would turn up in time to start at 2.30 exactly like any other team: tea 5, draw 6.45 or 7.15 if there was anything in it: then a glass of beer perhaps at the pub and a nice drive home to their quarters in the cool of the summer evening. They had heard much of our pretty village grounds which are unknown in Australia, all grass being burnt up by the heat, and were anxious to have a game on one. 'Oh yes, pass the word round certainly in surrounding villages, boys; but keep it to yourselves, you understand, all private like and incog.'

The news appeared first as a rumour (the match was entered X on the Tillingfold card), then the rumour was described as a hoax, which was fiercely denied. The British Broadcasting Corporation mentioned the matter in neat English with a courteous smile, and the world pricked up its ears. The thing suddenly became a gigantic stunt. The national game played in its natural surroundings: the village green is the home of cricket: a noble gesture illustrative of all that is finest in democracy: the snobbery of Test Matches: the fatal respect of persons degraded the freedom which was the birthright of every Briton ... There was no slogan, political or social or religious, that was not tacked somehow on to this little game. And astute financiers saw there was money in it: the suggestion was actually made that the game should be played by artificial light at Olympia. But the climax was reached when Mr. Hitler, who dictates to a neighbouring country, decided that here was the golden opportunity for his Nazis to learn about the great English game in its simplest yet grandest form: the running commentary translated into German was to be broadcast throughout the length and breadth of his Reich, to battalions of Nazis drawn up in ranks to listen. Pictures of the game, with elucidatory comment, were to be thrown on every screen: an intensive course of cricket culture (to be known always under drastic penalties as Hitler-ball) was arranged to start from this one game, which as I have said was intended to be a friendly and informal affair. The Soviet, French and Italian governments, growing suspicious, sent secret agents to investigate. Many serious persons wrote to serious papers urging the necessity of an international conference at Geneva to discuss all possible implications, before an encounter which might have such far-reaching consequences on world welfare should take place.

The effect of all this publicity upon the village team was both distressing and unpleasant. Tillingfold have, for one reason and another, experienced some difficulty in raising a side at all this season. This world-hubbub made it clear, as the great day drew nearer, that the difficulty of raising a side for this important match would be well-nigh insuperable. Natural diffidence caused our fellows to shrink from makin' monkeys of themselves, as one man put it: another man declined to be treated like a bloody film star and be paid nothing for his pains.

In consequence it became increasingly difficult to raise a side, but Mr. Gauvinier, faced with the ignominy of turning out one or even two men short when the eyes of the Empire were upon him, and of asking Mr. Woodfull to oblige with a couple of substitutes when the ears of the world were pricked to catch his voice, eventually succeeded in getting a fairly representative side together, even though he was seriously upset by receiving an urgent message marked Strictly Confidential from Headquarters, giving him a hint, large as the imprint of an elephant's foot and even weightier, as to the extreme inadvisability of employing in his attack upon the Australian batsmen anything even remotely resembling Leg Theory or anything that might possibly be construed into Leg Theory. In fact, under the circumstances, considering the unfortunate state of Japanese trade rivalry, it might be wiser perhaps to have no man at all, except a mid-on well

68

back, upon the leg-side, when the more important batsmen were at the wicket.

Thus an avalanche of extraneous matter descended upon the game and bade fair to wreck and bury it, as the snow thundering down the mountain-side may wreck and bury an Alpine village.

On Wednesday morning the ground looked peaceful and smiling in the sunshine as it usually looks of a fine morning: a few toddlers staggered about on the pleasant stretch of mown grass, as they usually do, greatly daring but not too far from their prams and their mothers. The square on which the wickets were to be pitched waited expectant, full of promise, full of that happy promise, which only a cricket ground packed with stored memories of good games won and good games lost can ever give in all its richness of unforgettable incident. On Wednesday afternoon came the first sign of what was to happen. A motor-car with trailer attached drew up by the gate leading into the ground: its occupants got out, looked round, saw a farmhouse near, called at the farm, and were seen to return, slowly drive car and trailer into the adjoining field and come to a slow stop. First one by one they came, then in twos, then in threes, and settled in the adjoining fields, as gipsies come from all over England to settle on the course at Epsom. By Friday the thing began to look serious: and the British Broadcasting Corporation kindly consented to make a statement in their news items to the effect that the cricket match which was undoubtedly to be played between Tillingfold and the Australians was essentially a friendly and intimate affair; that listeners should be reminded that the accommodation on a village ground was strictly limited, unlike Old Trafford or Trent Bridge or The Oval, where thousands could watch the play in comparative comfort. And so on and so on. The announcement was, of course, beautifully worded and exquisitely spoken, but its effect, however well intentioned, was unfortunate: for the average listener thought 'Oh that's all right, then: nobody will be turning up, so there'll be plenty of room for us.' And forthwith determined to make a day of it.

From every town within reach, moreover (and what town now is not within reach?), charabanc and coach proprietors prepared excursion parties (with lunch and tea included in the fare) to see the match. On Friday night the stream of traffic began to flow; early on Saturday morning it was in full spate; from North and West and East, converging upon Tillingfold; a vast concourse of vehicles. By midday there were evidences of such a traffic block as had hitherto been unknown in the short history of motoring. The Authorities, with the help of the A.A. and the R.A.C., did what they could, but they were powerless: our village policeman was wonderful, but what could one man effect against this national obsession? Mr. Gauvinier began to have serious fears that those of his team who went to work at any distance might be unable to reach their homes in time to have dinner and change: and that those who lived a mile or so outside the village would be unable to reach the ground at all. He was all right himself, as he could walk by field-paths most of the way; to bicycle, as was his usual practice, was quite out of the question. But what would others do? Just as he was leaving the house the telephone bell rang. He was thankful that he had not disconnected it, as rage and despair at its persistent ringing for the last twenty-four hours had prompted him to do; for it was Mr. Woodfull speaking. He was speaking from Shoreham. He had arranged not without difficulty to start an hour before his scheduled time but they were properly stuck at Shoreham. Dreadful. Yes. Have you heard? No. What, the Soviet? Yes, Stalin's mad Hitler's got the jump of him: when he's decreed days ago all good Russians must take to cricket. Sure? Oh yes, Foreign Office rang me up at 10.25. Oh we'll make it. Sure thing. And are you there? There's to be an American broadcast. Short-length wave. Yes. Sort of return for Kansas Derby. We'll get; but may be a trifle late. Some game. Yes. So long.

Mr. Gauvinier started on his walk to the ground, cursing the foolish circumstances which caused him, an oldish man, to start the afternoon with a one-and-a-half-mile's walk carrying a cricket bag. It seemed, too, a great shame that Italy, France and Spain should be left out, as they appeared to be. He'd had such a happy time in Florence, he was half French: he'd always wanted to visit Spain, the home of Don Quixote and Sancho Panza. But the sight of the country lane that he was obliged to cross and along which he usually bicycled quietly to the ground, scattered these altruistic broodings. It was, for as far as he could see, a solid jam of motor vehicles of every description, from baby cars to the most enormous coaches on which he had ever (having missed the last Motor Show) set his astonished eyes.

'You goin' to play in the match? Coo! Er! I'm comin' in tow!' Gauvinier pretended not to hear: but it was no good. The cry was taken up like magic or wireless loud-speakered, and soon a seething, struggling mob (squabbling too, for it was shouted in expostulation, 'How'll you ever find your way back to your seat and what'll you do then miles away from anywhere?') was swarming in his company along the shaded pathway, known as Lovers' Lane. He overheard: 'Some sort of souvenir, to show the kids,' and became aware how violent and infectious is mass emotion, for he began to feel, as he quickened his pace, that he had somehow ceased to be a person and become merely (trousers, shirt, coat, bag and bag's contents) a compendium of possible souvenirs, likely to be dispersed at any moment.

A label on his cricket bag did the mischief: 'It's Govineer, the village captain!' came an excited shout.

He broke into a run: they gave chase, yelling to him as tasty a morsel to his greedy pursuers as ever hare to hounds. Had he not, with great presence of mind, dropped his bag to leave them scrambling and struggling for its contents, it is doubtful what would have happened to him: probably what happens to a Russian traveller when overtaken by hungry wolves on the snow-clad steppes. As it was he reached the ground whole in body but ruffled in spirit, or rather he reached the next field but one adjoining the ground.

Tum demum, then and not till then (so slow is even a moderately intelligent mind to grasp a situation outside its previous experience), the full extent of the catastrophe, which publicity had wrought upon what should have been a rather specially good little game, broke upon his consciousness. He was in fact almost as nonplussed as the Higher Military Command by the events of the Great War. Like them he simply did not know what to do. He could only murmur to himself, as he threaded his difficult way through cars and campers and hundreds ever anxious to press somehow nearer to the field of play: 'All I know is this isn't cricket!' Bagless, bootless, batless, padless, capless, he eventually arrived at what had been the ground, and now resembled some weirdly arranged sort of car park: and he, the stickler for punctuality, heard the monastery clock chime three above the babel.

'Barely room for a tennis court,' he sadly thought. 'No room at all for Tim Wall's run—if he should get here.'

'This is an outrage, sir,' a furious voice accosted him. 'An absolute disgrace. Do you realize this is a great occasion? Are these the best arrangements you folk are capable of making? Have you no sense of responsibility, no glimmer of what is fitting?'

'Yes. Yes. But I've no cricket boots,' was all Gauvinier could say.

'Grossly selfish and personal! No thought for the good name of the country: no thought for her prestige in the eyes of other nations. You saunter on to the ground half an hour late. It's an infamy!'

'Yes. Yes. But I've no cricket boots,' Gauvinier sadly repeated.

'Something's got to be done about it: and pretty sharp, too!'

'Oh, I agree!' said Gauvinier. 'But I have never played without cricket boots before!'

High words might have arisen between the village captain and the enraged Broadcasting Official, had not, most fortunately, their attention been distracted by the manœuvres of an aeroplane flying uncommonly low.

'Gosh! It's an autogiro. Look, there are two of them.'

All looked up: and large numbers were bumped in the back as they gazed up by eager photographers rushing forward with their cameras. 'Not on the wicket, please,' the distraught Gauvinier supplicated at the top of his voice, still thinking only of his wretched little game. His pitiful cry was not heard: with dismay he watched first one, then the other, slowly and beautifully alight upon the wicket. The crowd surged nearer to see Mr. Woodfull emerge with his cricket bag from the first: Mr. Bradman from the second. The cameras clicked; millions next day read the caption: *This picture shows Mr. Woodfull arriving on the Tillingfold ground: eager for his encounter with the village.*

Mr. Gauvinier found himself shaking hands with Mr. Woodfull, and murmuring foolishly:

'Awfully sporting of you to have turned up. All this,' he

waved a rueful hand, 'I'm most dreadfully sorry about it. Such a pretty little ground: never very large: now it is rather close quarters, I'm afraid.'

And Mr. Woodfull, as behoves a visiting captain, remained dauntlessly courteous and cheerful, and assured him that he was certain they'd have a really jolly little game in spite of everything. Gauvinier shook a doubtful head.

'There's room perhaps to toss,' he said, extracting a half-crown from his trouser pocket. But even so simple and so pleasant a matter of routine as the toss was not permitted to take place without interference. On the instant two or three excited photographers leaped forward crying out: 'Just one moment, *please*!' in the harsh tone of authority curbing exasperation with incompetence. 'It's more usual for captains to toss in front of the pavilion in their cricket kits.'

'There is no front to the pavilion now: and I have no kit now . . .' Gauvinier mourned.

We may waive that. Now, left hand lightly placed in left trouser-pocket. So. Half-crown placed on right thumb-nail. So. Thank you. Your head turned slightly more this way. Mr. Woodfull, please if you would step two paces nearer. Thank you. Three-quarter face to the camera.' 'Perhaps both gentlemen would not mind removin' their Trilbies,' suggested another photographer. 'What about Mr. Bradman comin' into the picture?' a third suggested, which enraged a fourth who had been arranging to make a special and exclusive snap *Don Bradman watching the skippers toss*.

'Take us or leave us!' said Mr. Woodfull, unused to being thus hectored, bluntly to the photographers, and added kindly to Mr. Gauvinier: 'You just toss, old man.'

But Mr. Woodfull's attention was distracted at that moment by the return of the autogiros. The welfare of his men was near to his heart, as it should be to the heart of every sound captain.

'Pack up, you fellows,' he shouted unceremoniously. 'Out of the way. Make a larger space, there. They must have room to alight.'

And he started to signal frantically to the 'planes, waving his hat in one hand and his handkerchief in the other.

Meanwhile Mr. Bradman had slipped off, like the boy he is, merrily shouldering his way through the crowd, in search of coco-nut shies which he felt must be lurking in such precincts and for which he has a very great liking. He is accustomed to visit the fairs round Melbourne and Sydney in a small Ford van in which to take home his winnings, or if he should go with Mr. Kippax or Mr. McCabe, in a Leyland lorry. The proprietors of these and kindred forms of amusement were not the least thankful among Australian sportsmen when no untoward circumstance prevented the great Test team of 1934 from sailing for the shores of England.

Now, too, Mr. Gauvinier's arm was gripped by the same Broadcasting Official, by this time almost completely distraught.

'Something's got to be done about it,' he babbled. 'Something's got to be done about it. We can't go on describing the rural scene for ever. Nobody could.'

'I tried to toss,' Gauvinier excused himself.

'Such shocking management is a disgrace to the country. Do you mean to tell me an English crowd is so unsporting as to ruin the very thing they have come miles and at great personal inconvenience to see?'

'I've told you nothing,' Gauvinier said. 'You can see for yourself it looks uncommonly like it. No one man by himself would do it: a mass of men together does.'

However, by 4.30 the last of the village team had fought his painful way on to what was left of the ground, dishevelled certainly, but determined (fair play being fair play) not to be crowded out of his well-earned Saturday's game by any mob of gaping sightseers. This proper bulldog spirit took them to the ground and then deserted them. They stood about miserably, powerless to help Gauvinier clear a slightly larger space around the poor pitch. But Mr. Gauvinier, elated at having been at last allowed to toss and at having won it, raised his voice and appealed to the better nature of the crowd: and what man has ever made such an appeal to an English crowd in vain? By the time the last Australian, who happened to be Mr. Wall himself, arrived (engine trouble had delayed the gallant hop from Shoreham) Mr. Gauvinier was able to take him by the arm and show him how, with a little care, he might still have room for the full length of his admirable run to the wicket. This caused Mr. Gauvinier the very greatest satisfaction. Tea 7, draw 9. That was four hours. They'd get their little game. True, the ground was a bit confined and the autogiros had not improved the pitch: but, good Lord! one mustn't be fussy, and after all it would be the same for both sides, and a really sporting gentleman had returned him his boots and cap. Thus when just after five the Australians took the field (Sam Bird squeezing between motors had badly soiled his newly washed white umpire's coat) and Mr. Ballard and Mr. McLeod reached the wickets to bat, he felt almost at peace within and happy at the prospect of quite a decent little game, after all.

The crowd too were in the best of spirits. They appreciated being at such close quarters with the famous Australians, and felt quite safe, their glass screens being Triplex and suitably insured.

Mr. Woodfull adapted his field to the new conditions, and placed his men in a masterly manner, and with his well-known consideration for others arranged that after each ball his men should move one on in the small circle (more resembling Kiss-in-the-Ring perhaps than cricket) so that as many of the spectators as possible might have the joy of close proximity to all the great Australian players in turn.

But a large black cloud had been gathering, and as Mr. Wall, who was to open the bowling, began to walk slowly away to count the steps of his run, a drop (and it was a large one) fell upon his head. This caused him such surprise that he lost count and came slowly back to the wicket: and began once more. This time he reached the first car, which he was obliged to pass, and in it was now sitting a fair (and she was very fair) occupant. Mr. Wall stopped dead. The perfectly behaved English crowd turned their heads to one side or whispered 'Will it rain?' looking upwards, and to a man thought only what would have been shouted aloud by the rude barrackers on the Hill down under. They waited in respectful silence, broken at length by a clap of thunder and a sudden downpour of rain. It was a deluge. What man in the mass had failed to stop, the weather had. Over every other trick of fate these lion-hearted fellows had prevailed: but with the weather even cricketers themselves, like Gods with stupidity, fight in vain.

No European incident occurred. Mr. Hitler and Mr. Stalin remained quite unperturbed; and wholly satisfied with the 'phoned apologies of the Foreign Office, each addressed their young men, without a moment's hesitation, upon the duties of Nazi and Communist citizenship respectively. The young men had heard this before many times, but drawn up in ranks, as they were, at any rate they were temporarily kept from that mischief which another would-be dictator, Mr. Satan, is always anxious to find for idle hands (even when attached to Nazi or Communist wrists) to do.

So in the end all turned out really for the best in what is probably (though weather, women and what-not might conceivably be improved) the best of all possible worlds.

TILLINGFOLD *V*. GRINLING GREEN

(*To Walter Charman*)

A SMALL group of men were standing silent and thoughtful upon the ground at Tillingfold, looking at the turf with serious mournful eyes. It was the Public Recreation Ground—a large field, a big slice of which was weekly mown by a kindly General's motor mower for the benefit of the Cricket Club. On this mown slice, the children gambolled, youths from the Tile Works played single wicket and rounders, prams and go-carts were wheeled and everyone was happy. Everyone, that is, except the Tillingfold Cricket Club, famous among neighbouring cricket clubs, who strove valiantly against fearful odds to get a decent wicket for their matches every Saturday.

A few optimists had rejoiced to hear the Council had at last taken the matter in hand. Money had been voted by the Council—marvel of marvels—to be spent on the ground. Their hopes were rudely dashed. Nice new benches were installed; the turf of the square received a sprinkling of dressing; and the mown area remained the same large patch in an incipient hayfield.

'It might be perfect. Room for all,' groaned Gauvinier for the many hundredth time.

'It keeps me awake at nights! Really. I can't sleep for thinking of those lads racing about in them great boots till ten of a night!'

'Well, why isn't something done about it?' asked Ballard, a new-comer, cheerfully.

Old-timers who knew the history of the Club's struggles to survive looked at him and shook their heads, solemnly chuckling. Nothing was said.

Sam Bird, the umpire, felt the topic was too painful. He slowly tried to change it and failed, saying in his careful manner:

'I am pleased we are playing Grinling Green. They are a very good side, I am told. Sir Arthur Crowly takes great

77

interest in cricket, and their ground in his park is a little beauty. Mown all round.' The eyes of the group travelled sadly over the rough hayworthy outfield.

'Oh blast you, Sam!' laughed Gauvinier.

And they set about doing the best they could with what they had, which is certainly more sensible than unhappily dreaming of what so easily might be, but is not—yet.

And on Saturday afternoon the wicket, dead soft after summer rain, had rolled out none too badly. And, though the sky was overcast, there was a distinct promise of a break in the clouds and eventual sunshine.

The Tillingfold team strolled up, more casually even than usual, to hide their excitement at meeting strong new opponents with a big name; anxious to do themselves and Tillingfold justice. Several tried to ease their tense feelings by remarking: 'Win or lose. Don't matter a hoot! So long as it's a good game.' Which is perfectly true. It is also perfectly true that it is, somehow, more satisfactory to win.

Others remarked, with British unconcern: 'After all it's only a bit of sport. That's what I say!' Without any doubt it was as well that nobody knew the sort of game they were in for.

Tillingfold are a good little side this season, keen and safe in the field, with a tail that can wag and five or six batsmen who can make runs quickly on their day—an essential where time stands always a relentless second opponent in every match and the players must be keyed up for a sprint, not trained for an endurance trial.

Gauvinier noticed the eleventh man cycling down the hill from the village as a small motor-bus slowed up by the ground and pushed tentatively in at the gate.

The visiting team had arrived and the players emerged backwards from the old blue bus—among them, to Gauvinier's joy, an old friend, Slater, who used to captain Raveley some years ago—a left-handed batsman who could hit like a kicking mule, never dropped a catch and could bowl a decent ball. The other faces were strange, but they looked a likely lot.

They had an air of quiet confidence about them which was most impressive. Some teams on arrival do impart respect. And Gauvinier, searching to discover their skipper, was quick to feel this and to wonder what effect Tillingfold produced, visiting a strange ground.

Grinling Green played matches on the County ground at Horsham. So had Tillingfold for that matter, on one occasion, with a Wednesday team, alas! having beaten a good Horsham side one Bank Holiday with their sound Saturday team.

Search for the skipper was interrupted by badinage with Slater, that he should still be turning out at his extreme old age—a delicate subject for one who would never see fifty again and was looking in vain for a new pair of bellows:

'Don't you bury me yet,' Gauvinier laughed. 'But seriously, who is your skipper?'

'Well, that I don't rightly know. Our usual skipper's not playing, y'see. Who's skippering, Jack?'

'Oh, ask Bill, there.'

'You're a nice lot! A bunch of sheep straggling round. . . .'

'Well. The truth is we never know till a Friday mornin' who's coming from the House, if you take my meaning. Rather messes things up. There's our old vicar turning up'— (he pointed to a car making its way through the gate on to the ground). 'Rare old sportsman, he is. Thirty year and more been with us. Shouldn't wonder if his boy weren't skipper. That nice kid, there, with the sandy hair.'

Gauvinier saw a man approach the boy and heard:

'Will you run the side for us to-day, Mr. Bakewell?'

'Certainly. Delighted,' the boy answered, blushing.

Gauvinier stepped up to him.

'Let's toss then, shall we? You shout.'

The boy called 'heads' and heads it was.

'We'll bat,' he said, without a smile or a moment's hesitation.

'Tea five? Draw seven?' Gauvinier put the usual query.

'Right,' said the boy, strung up to his responsibility, and strode away with a tense face to make out his order of batting.

'Fancy letting a nipper like that beat you for the toss!' laughed Slater. 'Never could do that job, could you?'

'You wait! You wait!'

Gloomy sky, bad light, a wicket soft as mud—anything might happen.

The field were in their places. The batsmen came in, resolute fellows, both of them, accustomed, you felt sure, like Holmes and Sutcliffe, to many a good opening partnership.

Ballard, beginning the bowling, knew how to keep a good length and could turn the ball both ways. The first over was a maiden, each ball a good one, played with quiet sureness. Gauvinier found the other man as watchful and as sure. He took a well-run single off his last ball. They could both bat as well as look like batsmen.

Ballard's first ball, shortish on the leg stump, was nicely put for an easy two. His next was a good one, had the batsman guessing, came in inches from the off and missed the wicket by a fraction—a beauty. Another like that, you could see him thinking, but it was shorter and was hit hard towards cover.

They started to run. 'No! Wait!' Freddie Winthrop at cover nipped along to the ball at a surprising pace, gathered it cleanly and whipped it in. Second thoughts were best when trying to steal anything like a short run from Freddie. The field exchanged smiles, well knowing and very proud of Freddie's cat-like quickness and the slight resentment that appeared on his face at any liberty.

Tillingfold were a pretty useful fielding side. Another proof of it. Tall Dick Culvert at point jumped out and down at a hard square cut and stopped it so that the batsman felt robbed of three sure runs. Good work. This was going to be some game. Mid-off and mid-on returned the remaining balls of the over, carefully played, to the bowler.

Gauvinier liked a wicket with a little fire in it—he liked a hot sun. This mud heap took all sting out of every ball. The pitch was so soft that the fellow could play back to a good-length ball with apparent safety and did so four times running —no one could if the wicket were decently hard. A slower one, then, pitched farther up, might fool him out perhaps. Yes. Two minds. He'd fumbled it. The off stump leaned delightfully back. The first wicket, and a good one, had fallen for three runs.

In came Slater with his usual smile, left-handed, a nuisance, though a very genial one. Gauvinier knew him of old—a good man to see the back of. He always attacked the bowling from the very start, quick on his feet to step out and drive a good-length ball; quick, too, to step back and hook a shortish one. And he hit very hard, as the fieldsmen were soon to discover. But not quite yet. The wicket had fallen to the last ball of the over.

The Grinling Green Sutcliffe faced Ballard, who tempted him with a cunning slow but tempted him in vain. He played it carefully back to mid-off. A horrid thing happened off the next ball, which poor Gauvinier will remember for some time; for he fancied himself at short slip and had held some good ones in his time. It was well-pitched up and very much faster. Snick, lowish to his right hand—a beauty to get—a pig to drop; and he dropped it. He cursed to himself and called out his sorrow to the bowler. His mind was wandering to Slater. Deuce take it, all excuses are lies. It was a maiden over, with no semblance of another chance.

'Oh, sorry, I bowl round the wicket to a left-handed man.'

And the umpire gave Slater another guard. He drove the first ball hard along the ground past mid-on to the man in the deep. All the fieldsmen noticeably sat up, looking forward (and rightly) to a merry time.

'Right hand!' Gauvinier sang out, and waited for Sam Bird to push at a wary toddle across to his place. He would give it up soon if there were any stand and remain bashfully at point; but not quite yet.

Followed two decent balls at which the batsman played forward and just failed to flick into slip's hand. The next one, shortish, he square cut hard past point for two. A lucky snick past his leg stump gave them one more. And Slater drove the last ball hard by cover, who stopped it with a dexterous foot but could not save the run.

Slater faced Ballard for the first time, who immediately gave him a tempting one. The temptation was not resisted. Slater let drive and lifted it just short of the deep field, who saved the second run. A short one on the leg stump was put away for two: Ballard's first really loose ball. Dodging about first one side of the wicket, then the other, to this infernal left-hander, thought Gauvinier. It looked as if the two were going to stop there and make runs. But Ballard did not like presenting a batsman with runs. His last ball had been a gift. His next ball was a corker. It broke in half a foot from the off and smashed down the off stump. Right out of the basket, that one. Had the batsman guessing all the way. Two for eleven, of which the man retiring had made eight.

Entered a large friendly boy, a little stouter than seemed quite necessary, but he very soon showed the knowing that he could bat. He watched the ball off the pitch and played it with a straight bat, very straight. Nor could Ballard fool him with his change of pace. He finished the over smiling and confident, remarking to Gauvinier at the end of it, very nicely: 'He does mix 'em up, sir, doesn't he?'

At Gauvinier's first ball Slater took a mighty dip, thinking no doubt a six into the road would freshen the air a bit, but he completely missed the ball and laughed happily when he realized the ball had missed the wicket. He lofted the next towards Jack Small at deep mid-wicket, who came haring in, but it was well outside even that fleet fieldsman's reach.

'Dashed if I can get hold of 'em to-day!' he confided, panting, to Gauvinier. 'But I'll get you into the pond yet. See if I don't.' He referred to a pond on the far side of the road in which many a good Tillingfold ball had been sunk.

'That pond's been many a one's undoing!' laughed Gauvinier reminiscently, preparing to bowl to the large friendly boy. He began to play forward, changing his mind, and came down hard on the ball in the nick of time; a shot only possible, Gauvinier groaned to realize, on a dead pitch, soft as mud. The large boy realized it too, for he looked quite clearly happy to be still at the wicket.

A slower one and we'll have him c and b, thought Gauvinier. It was slower, right enough, but short and the boy tapped it for one. Slater let fly at the next, missed his hit again but flicked it for a single. The last ball, a fast one, hit the large boy's leg, which seemed to Gauvinier, who appealed loudly, bang in front of the middle stump. But the visiting umpire thought otherwise and the appeal was disallowed. Opinions often do differ. A very good fellow, the umpire, but with a heart a little too warm, perhaps, for the young chaps of his side.

A bye brought Slater back. He didn't believe in pottering about and getting cold. Not a bit of it. Batting for him meant exercise and excitement. Hit or miss, his every shot showed immense bodily vigour. He jumped out at the ball almost before it had left Gauvinier's hand, then checked himself with a superb effort and played it, laughing, straight back to the bowler. The next he pulled hard to mid-wicket, where Jack Small by his speed saved two.

Singles came during the next two overs, with the feeling

strong in both bowlers and most of the fieldsmen that any ball to Slater might be a sudden six. If he once began to see them properly, he would keep the boys busy shifting the numbers on the score-board. He hadn't hit a good one yet and was becoming impatient. Gauvinier bowled a tempting slower one to his impatience, saw him take a tremendous dip at it, right across and far too soon, saw the stumps gently displaced. And the Tillingfold boys had a better little job than Slater would have found them, as they hung up 19—3—8 on the board.

And they were kept busy in this most satisfactory way. For, though the large boy was playing soundly and the short elderly newcomer obviously knew how to use a bat, just as the latter was getting nicely at home he played a short one from Gauvinier that shot hard on to his wicket: 25—4—2. And in his next two overs Ballard cleaned bowled two men— one with a beauty that came in from the off, and the young skipper, who, in his eagerness to lift his side out of the rut, hit across a half-volley. Six wickets were down for twenty-eight runs.

It looked pretty good for Tillingfold and many spectators thought they had got the great Grinling Greeners beaten all ends up. But the large friendly boy stuck manfully to it and the remaining batsmen clung on to give him all the support they could. One hit, to the sorrow of Tillingfold, who prided themselves on their fielding, went straight through mid-off's legs to the boundary. The bowling was changed and a full toss was hit to the pavilion for another four. The score mounted: 37 for 7—44 for 8—54 for 9, the last wicket falling at fifty-five, the large boy carrying out his bat for as useful a twenty-five as he can ever hope to make.

And fifty-five would take a lot of getting on that treacherous soft pitch, with the dreadful snail-slow impervious outfield.

Ted Griffiths and Ballard opened the Tillingfold innings after the trusty groundsman had sadly done his best with broom and roller to make the sorry wicket playable.

Everyone watched tensely to see what the bowling was like—those agonizing first balls. The elderly short man bowled to Ted Griffiths. No run to speak of, a low action, using his height the wrong way on, as it were, to keep low. A bye, a single off the bat—he seemed to offer little difficulty to Ted except for one that shot (a horrid warning of what was to come), down on to which Ted came like a hammer.

From the other end a thick youth bowled, winding himself up to deliver the ball on a curious shuffling run. A full toss. Ballard, surprised at the sudden sweetness of the gift, failed in his effort to hit the ball over the pavilion. It glanced off his leg for one. The thick youth did not wish—stout fellow—to be partial with his favours. He gave Ted a full toss, which the long grass and deep mid-wicket prevented between them from being more than one run.

Ballard drove his next one past cover, a beautifully timed shot which deserved more than two. There was a distinct easing of the tenseness in the atmosphere. This bowler looked dead easy—too dead easy, alas! Ballard took a dip at a half-volley, hit across it and the ball seemed to stick in the softness of the pitch, rise straight and slowly most wickedly to tip the off bail to the ground. It trembled on the top of the stumps and fell. But though it fell wavering like a feather on to the grass, it fell like a lump of lead on to the spirits of the team and of the Tillingfold supporters: 5—1—2 looked horrid on the score-board. Horrid bad when Ballard was the man that was out.

Spirits revived as Alec John strode sturdily in. Not an orthodox bat but with a marvellous eye. Made a lot of runs, too, and liked a slow wicket. He seemed, by the way he played his first few shots, to be seeing them all right. But then came a long hop which he hit hard and straight into the hands of mid-off. 5—2—0. Hang it all! It was going to be a procession.

'Not if I know it!' thought Jimmie Harrison as he walked out hurriedly, with a half-smile on his face, to the wickets. He was shy in manner but resolute in action. And he started playing from the first ball he got with ease and confidence, as though there could be no danger whatever that the runs would not be hit off. Meantime old Ted was content to dig himself in, taking not the shadow of any risk, though he dearly loved to have a dip, often his undoing. You could see his grim smile from the pavilion, amused at his own restraint.

The bowlers were giving nothing away now, but Jimmie worked the score up to ten with good shots. And then, just as anxiety was beginning to lessen a little, Ted tried to drive the elderly short bowler, got the ball on the edge of his bat and was well caught by Slater at third man: 11—3—2.

Tillingfold's spot boy, young Jack, whom everyone wanted to see coached at the County Nursery, was the next man in.

Jimmie Harrison continued to bat as though he were quite capable of making the few runs wanted off his own bat. He seemed to become only more confident when the short bowler, who was keeping nastily low, missed his off stump by inches with a deadly shooter. Young Jack, too, after an early lapse was getting them in the centre of his bat. Watching them like a cat, too, he came down hard on a beast that kept abominably low. Runs came. Twenty went up. The excitement became painful, and a roar went up when Jack swept a half-volley to leg for four—a lovely smack, beautifully timed. The next one went for a couple. Things were moving.

But Jimmie, facing the short bowler, was not to be hurried into taking any risk. He was bowling very straight and very well and needed a lot of watching for the ball that came in low. Only a single off that over. The tenseness tightened again unbearably. Each took a single off the other bowler who was putting down some poor stuff. A bye sent up thirty. It was anybody's game. Jack got a beauty for two which ought to have been four. Two more singles—the score was mounting. Jack faced the wily little man, forgot his horrid habit of keeping low, went out to drive him to the boundary, the ball got under his bat and hit his leg stump—34—4—13, that thrice unlucky number.

Tall Dick Culvert strode in, glancing back at the score-board. Six more for forty, then fifty. Why, of course, the runs would be got, and he'd have a deuced good try to get some of 'em. Watch out for that low ball. Why, dash it! There was nothing to it.

He played the first ball perfectly—if it had shot dead, he would have had it—but alas! the next one bumped up. There was a loud appeal. He was out, caught at the wicket: 34—5—0.

Gauvinier, in spite of the sad fact that he would never see fifty again, was absurdly shaking with excitement as he pulled off his sweater to go in. He strode out, urging himself to curb his quite senseless impatience, trying to convince himself that the thought how a couple of sixes would change the look of things was a rash thought and unwise. Wait for the loose ones! Wait for the loose ones! he repeated again and again.

Middle and leg. Ah, good! The first was an easy one. He played it past mid-off for an unhurried single and he had the bowling again. Joy! A long hop on the off, no extra cover. It went hard and true—a four but for that accursed long grass —a two as it was, meaning some forty yards' sprint, curse it! And he was reminded how badly he needed a new pair of bellows, which no store, however universal, could supply.

A sharpish single set him panting. Still, runs were runs. And oh Lord! here's Jimmie hitting another two. The pace was furious, but forty was being put up on the score-board, a heartening sight. Then a single, a sharp one, and leaning on his bat to recover a bit he reflected that every run was, after all, a day's march nearer home.

He shook his white head, smiling, at the wicket-keeper, who remarked kindly: 'Take your time!'

No more runs that over, though the bowler had a lovely drive to stop and was cheered for stopping it. The pace slowed down. A single each. Nearing fifty, anyhow. No need to hurry. Then another two past cover for Gauvinier, who began to realize that there was such a thing as second wind. Jimmie and he would pull it off all right now. He watched Jimmie with contentment play a good one safely back—watched him take his stance for the next, moving forward to back well up as the bowler moved. Look at that! The ball shot dead in from outside the off stump on to the middle stump. Jimmie was bowled, as most people would have been, neck and crop: 47—6—16. The last ball of the over. They surely were fairly safe. And a new bowler was being put on.

Same guard. Glory! a full toss. Gauvinier, too eager to paste it out of the ground, hit too quick and played it with the extreme end of his bat, a fantastically ridiculous shot. Such a gift rejected! But the new bowler was kind or nervous. Followed a long hop on the off, beaten for two. The forty yards' sprint was a distinct punishment for missing that gift of a watched six. And Gauvinier, rattled by the miss, was ass enough to stand for the next ball before he had recovered his breath. In consequence he mishit a half-volley, skying the ball to Slater at third man, who judging it perfectly brought off a better catch even than his first: 49—7—12. Or six for a tie and seven for a win.

Also it was past five o'clock and tea-time. And there was Freddie Winthrop out, caught in the slips.

They adjourned for tea at 49—8—0: six being wanted for a tie and seven for a win.

Being true-born Britons, the players of Tillingfold and Grinling Green found the position of the game interesting and in no wise allowed it to interfere with the enjoyment of bread-and-butter and cake and cups of tea. No sign of excitement appeared on any British face. One said to another: 'It's a good game, isn't it?' And the other replied: 'Yes. It is.' With an occasional exception, like spurts of fire, betraying the inner agitation. Freddie Winthrop, for instance, who had got out directly after Gauvinier, came up to him and said in a tense whisper: 'Sorry, Skipper. That was a—silly shot I got out with!' The chat was jerky and flowed less fully and freely than usual. Sid Smith, with his pads on, a picture of bulldog unconcern, spoke not at all. Gauvinier was keenly aware of his own French extraction. He gulped weak tea and smoked. Foolish, very foolish, but large slices of bread-and-butter and bun seemed out of place.

The youthful skipper of Grinling Green said shyly: 'A good little game, isn't it? Ought to be time for another knock each.'

'Oh well, hardly that, perhaps!' Gauvinier laughed, little knowing what time would bring forth.

Tea continued, longer it seemed and more imperturbably slow than ever.

At length tea ended and the men strolled out into the field —in more leisurely, more casual fashion than usual. The tail had often wagged before most usefully. Would it today? Not a shake. Not a wriggle. Two balls from the short elder bowler finished it off. Tillingfold were beaten by six runs—a spiritless, depressing finish.

The two skippers talked.

'Well! it's been a good little game. Most exciting!'

'May as well play right on.'

'Yes. And the sun's breaking through.'

Tillingfold went out into the field again.

'Look here! Let's dodge them out and knock off the runs.'

'Not an earthly.'

'But it's worth trying.'

'All right, we'll go all out for it.'

'Seriously it's about a hundred to one against us. Those fellows can bat.'

Gauvinier saw the youthful skipper going to his father's car as the two men came in to bat. The batting order was changed. There was an hour and three-quarters left for play.

Ballard bowled the first over, in which he took two wickets with clinking balls that nipped in from the off. It was clear that there was no definite policy. One man played anxious to make runs quickly; another played to win by the clock. Gauvinier bowled two maidens and took himself off. Slater came in, certain that a few boundaries would settle the matter. He skied the second ball and was caught.

The wickets were falling. There was a chance, still—a sporting chance. Gauvinier kept changing the bowling. Put on Alec John, who tossed up innocuous slows, at Ted's suggestion. A frightful risk. Alec's first ball was driven hard back. He leapt up, the gallant little Scot, and brought off a brilliant catch. Nothing went wrong. Every catch was held. Previous excitement was the merest shiver to the thrill the game was now creating.

Grinling Green began to realize how serious matters were getting. Seven wickets were down. And a first-wicket batsman, held in reserve, came in to stop this foolishness. He took no chances. Played a solid safe game. The hands of the enemy clock moved on. No thought of runs now. Simply stop there and win the game. Maiden followed maiden. Ah! At last, couldn't resist a smack at Alec. Freddie held a nice catch at extra cover. Eight wickets down. Three-quarters of an hour to go and twenty-five runs only to make. Two more tense overs and Ballard bowling the other end got a wicket. Only one more to go. A boy came in. It seemed as good as finished. But they both played with a dead straight bat, content to keep up their wickets. Over followed over. The minutes moved inevitably by. Gauvinier went on again himself and was starting to bowl his third ball when he saw the youthful skipper coming out on to the field from his father's car, not from his men in the pavilion. Gauvinier bowled. Returned to find the boy by him.

'We'll declare after this over,' he heard.

'But, my dear chap . . .' he began. 'Just wait one moment.'

He bowled, racking his brains how to tell the boy he *must* consult his team. Perhaps he had. And, anyhow, you couldn't teach a rival skipper his job, however nice a boy he was. He came back.

'We declare after this over,' the boy repeated.

'Frightfully sporting!' Gauvinier said. And let it go at that, praying that he might get that last wicket in one of the remaining balls. But it was not to be.

And Tillingfold left the field, bewildered, foiled and desperately keen to take the chance thus recklessly offered them.

Two wickets fell immediately. Ballard and Ted were too anxious to see a six soar out of the ground into the pond. Their places were taken, pretty well on the run. Alec John mishit and was caught. Jimmie was firm and unflurried as he had been in the first innings. Twos came. Sharp ones Throats cracked when he lifted a ball into the hedge for four. Twelve; fourteen. Jack Small hit a couple of twos and, bowled, ran out.

Gauvinier, going in one earlier, took his place. Roars greeted every run. Shouts of joy when the bowler hurled the ball at the wicket thinking to run out Gauvinier, backing right up. Jimmie pasted the ball past cover—ran like fury to turn an easy couple into three. Gauvinier staggered in to hear the wicket-keeper remark, 'Oh, pity! That's wrong!' and panting turned to see Jimmie waiting to know if the decision held.

Tall Dick ran in. They practically played tip and run. Twenty went up. Gauvinier's knees nearly gave under him, after a fast couple. The pace was furious. Last over was called. Another two; and another one. Two more. Good lord! They must have won. Two more singles. They couldn't slacken off.

The umpire removed the bails, pulled up the stumps. The game was over. They walked in, old Gauvinier pretty well speechless with the pace and the excitement.

The boy skipper had realized his mistake, if not from the mouths of his team, at any rate from their faces. He looked troubled. Gauvinier, as soon as he could root himself up from his seat by the score-board, found him by his father's car. He shook his hand in farewell, thanking him for a fine game.

'The most sporting declaration I've ever known,' he said, and was obliged to add, smiling: 'Almost too sporting, you know.'

HIS LAST GAME

(*To H. N. Best*)

H. N. B.   *What! more tripe, I suppose!*
H. de S.   *Yes, Harry: and more sauce from you—always, I hope, always.*

§ 1

GAUVINIER was always a superstitious dog; not in a nice, ordinary, sensible way like most of us, who dislike to see the new moon through glass or to walk under a ladder or sit down thirteen at table: but in his own rather peculiar way: attractive, if you liked him: annoying, most annoying, if you didn't. It was too queer and mystical, almost religious, if you understand me, inferring definitely the existence of powers other than human, and yet not naming them, not specifying them, giving you nothing you could bluntly contradict; leaving it all in the air. 'Well, there it is. What about it?' he'd say. 'Queer, at any rate, isn't it?' And he'd open his hands as no Englishman does and shrug his shoulders, his whole long expressive body one vibrant expressive question mark. You had to agree, it was queer.

And nothing was queerer than this his last game of cricket, certainly the last game in 1930, probably the last in his life. He may have insisted too much on his queerness: I am inclined to think that on the whole he did; but this I can say: if I had not known him pretty well and watched every ball of the game bowled, I should not have believed it. I mean this: if I had been writing a cricket yarn (and I have written one or two) I should have been obliged to tone the thing down, if you understand, to make it credible: this last game of his was a little too good to be true. However, it is well known that life can beggar art: and I vouch for the truth of this story; everyone in Tillingfold will vouch for it too. Ask anyone.

§ 2

I happened to be in the *Black Rabbit* on Monday evening when Gauvinier came striding in (the beggar's always in a

91

hurry, somehow) for the Selection Committee which met at eight. He looked worried, startled, as it were, and more tense even than usual.

'Hullo, Sam!' he called out to Sam Bird. 'No one here yet, then.'

Sam Bird slowly placed his glass of beer on the table and said slowly: 'Good evening, Captain. No. No one but you and me, at present. There seems a slight tardiness, if I may say so, on the part of the members of our Selection Committee.'

And he chuckled ponderously, as Sam always enjoys proofs of the imperfection of this imperfect world of ours, benignantly noticed by himself in others.

Gauvinier ordered a double brandy, and fidgeting nervously about (one or two strangers were sitting in the bar-parlour) at length said to me:

'Oh! come on: let's wait in the other room. Come on, Sam.' And stalked off into the billiard-room. I waited for old Sam, who never, never hurried, to push himself out from behind his marble-topped table and rise. I leant over him during the operation (unwittingly thereby stopping it) to say:

'There's something on his chest this evening.'

Sam pushed himself back, staring up at me.

'Our captain, sir,' he at length announced, 'is apt to take things too much to heart. A leetle too much to heart.'

I laughed agreement, and followed Sam into the billiard-room, where Gauvinier was sitting by the window. We sat by him. No one spoke. The silence was thick and awkward. Something was in the air other than the normal vagaries of the cricket club which Sam Bird wisely considered he was inclined to take too much to heart.

At length Gauvinier leaned forward and said, smiling without much fun in his smile, smiling shyly to hide his feeling:

'I've rather bad news, I'm afraid: damned bad so far as I am concerned. We've been swindled out of practically all our money. We've got to let the place. Clear out. Next Saturday will be my last game of cricket for many a long day.'

Sam Bird turned slowly round and stared. His face showed blank incomprehension. A first-class bit of news, good or bad, has its savour of satisfaction in the telling. The effect on Sam was prodigious. It obviously surprised Gauvinier, more sensitive than most men to feeling. He pressed Sam's arm. 'It might be worse: we shall have enough to live on.'

I felt devilish uncomfortable.

Sam slowly recovered speech and finding difficulty in enunciating each word, yet said: 'I trust things may turn out to be better than they now seem.'

'No: small hope of that, I fear: the bottom's out of the bucket, all right.'

And as he told us briefly of the American share-pushers' ingenious activities it seemed more than likely that it was.

He ended up: 'Upon my soul it's more like an Edgar Wallace novel than real life. Anyhow, it boshes up cricket for me: we don't quite know where we shall be or what we shall do.'

Gloom descended on us. Sam Bird's large face visibly swelled and reddened.

'That's the worst piece of news I've heard for a long time,' he said; 'yes, for a very . . . very long time.'

'Bad for the club,' I said.

'Ah!' Sam shook his head slowly from side to side. 'And worse than that!'

'Oh well!' Gauvinier laughed. 'Rotten for me. As for the club, a change is always good. Lord! I'd have hung on till I was kicked out. And I couldn't have gone on playing much longer, anyhow. I'd become a sort of habit, don't you know, that was a nuisance and yet couldn't be broken. It's snapped now all right. Probably the best thing that could have happened.'

'You'll be missed,' said the staunch Sam with conviction.

'For a little. For a little. But no man's indispensable, though he likes to think he is.'

It was getting a little too painful. Gauvinier had been skipper for pretty well ten years: had always been dead keen: never easy to run a side. His obvious faults dwindled: other things loomed rather larger. He had certainly done his best. I was glad when he broke the extreme discomfort of the moment by saying:

'Well, no one else seems likely to turn up. Let's get on with it.' He pulled out a pencil and paper.

'Lord! What luck for me. That this last game should be the best.'

For we were playing the General's team, which is always

the game of the season. This game was crucial, too, among that series of games, for as Sam Bird, ever an authority on statistics, begged leave to point out, eight matches had been played between the General's team and the village, of which each side had won four. Also we had won that season every match to date, and the wish not to be beaten was exceedingly strong.

'Pray for a fine day!' said Gauvinier, writing down a list of names. 'Wish you were fit,' he said to me.

'Wish I were,' I answered.

'Pretty decent side we've got this year,' he muttered, scanning the list.

'We'll need 'em, too,' chuckled Sam. 'If what I am informed is true.' His voice went up in its scale as he lifted his head to add almost perkily, rubbing his hands together with enormous satisfaction:

'I am informed that the General has some pretty useful players turning out for him—some pretty useful players.'

'As long as we put up a decent show,' I said. 'It's too sickening when we get caught on the run: diddled out for nothing.'

Sam Bird could not refrain from his stock remark.

'Cricket, gentlemen, is an uncertain game.'

Mine host, Alec John, successor to the famous Wishfort, came up and said in his beguiling Scottish (such a pleasant foreign language on his tongue):

'We'll be needing a guid side this week, y'know. We must *not* go down on Saturday, General or no General.'

Sam Bird began to announce the bad news.

'Our good captain here tells me . . .' and gave the gist of the sad story.

'Hoots! Ye don't say!' said Alec John, grieving, and it was clear that the prospect of the skipper's departure was affecting him as it had affected me, wiping out his faults and throwing a rosy light on other things.

Old Gauvinier stared in front of him. He didn't like it at all, any of it. Poor old blighter! It had got him fairly on the raw. You could see that.

'Pray that it's a fine day,' he repeated, and actually consented to have another small brandy with me: he's queer in his drinking as in most other things.

'How's that for a side?' he asked. 'Any change to suggest?'

Two or three men were mentioned and discussed: one change agreed upon.

'Lord!' he said, tipping down his brandy. 'I would like to take a wicket or two; and hit one more six.'

And his long legs hurried him out of the billiard-room.

§ 3

There was considerable talk in the village, as you can imagine, about the ill fortune which had fallen upon the Gauviniers. Many people had come and gone of late years. They had come and stopped on and seemed likely to stop on, indefinitely. Nice quiet people, the Gauviniers, generally liked. His immense keenness on cricket was remembered: his failings forgotten. His star rose on the horizon. We had got used to the old beggar somehow: and it seemed hard to believe at the moment that he wouldn't be playing again. Matches he'd pulled out of the fire came back to us: matches he'd lost by keeping himself on to bowl too long were forgotten.

One said to another with growing devoutness: 'My God! I hope the old beggar comes off on Saturday.' It gradually became a formulated and immense wish, comic in its urgency, that he should come off, that the match should be a good match and won.

Unthinkable, if after winning every match during the season, this last game—the crucial one, too, in the General's series—should be lost. Unthinkable. Feeling about it ran high.

I went up to see him during the week—on Thursday evening, as a matter of fact. He'd been twice up to town on business: and if ever a man looked bothered, he did. Something more than finance was preying on his mind.

I said to him, 'Look here. You've *got* to come off on Saturday.'

'Not a dog's chance, my dear chap! By rights I shouldn't play at all. This sort of thing shows a man up. See. A proper firm-lipped big-chinned white man would bow to the burden, shoulder it and march steadily forward, leading his women-folk to the new Promised Land.'

(He laughed and peered into me with his intense eyes.)

'I'm more like a stoated rabbit. A bundle of nerves. Damned if I *can* sleep. Every bush, every flower in this blasted place seems to have rooted in my heart. And other things: other things. . . . But, anyhow, I shall play on Saturday, though I shall be a passenger and nothing more. Must have one more game.'

He looked away.

'And always one has to wait and see. Things drag on. This to consider. That to think of. Nothing clean cut and definite in life.'

We walked round the garden. It certainly is an enchanting little place, the garden; all flowers and lawns which Gauvinier zealously mowed—beautifully set in a birch-wood.

'We've made it all ourselves. A keeper's cottage, added to. Pretty well waste land, except for the sunk garden, when we came.'

Then he switched off suddenly: ran into the house to fetch chairs and beer. We sat down in front of the house in the setting sun, on the brick pavement, the light playing on a mass of roses rambling in front of us over a pergola above beds, a flame of colour: a lovely sight: and he talked.

I am always interested, gripped rather, when Paul Gauvinier talks, though I defy any man to follow more than a quarter of what he says, when he gets going. He leaps from one subject to another: words pour from him: every word means something to him, and means it so intensely, that you are momentarily convinced it must mean something to you, too, and nod out emphatic *Yes-quite-wells* to his perpetual *You-see-what-I-mean?*, swept along by his queer intensity.

I came away after about an hour of it (very glad I had looked him up, though at first I felt intruding upon private sadness a little beyond my experience), my head reeling with his talk. Cricket, poetry, like, what mattered in life—money, love, affection, what *was* spiritual, what *was* material: how in one sense nothing mattered, how in another the littlest, most insignificant action might catch the light of, be the symbol of, all that was mightiest and most important: that he believed in Luck less than ever.

'But you mark my words, the end isn't written to this chapter yet. Queer things have always happened in my life.

Queer things always will happen to me. Cricket's only a game, I know: and it's physically impossible I could come off —but if I did . . . And, anyhow, I'll enjoy that game, however much of a fool I may make of myself. Aha! the whole game of life. Fail or not fail. And anything's better than to dry rot at ease till Judgment Day. Though this is a bit too exciting for my quiet taste.'

A queer fish, far too excitable, but I've always liked him. I shall not soon forget the way he said, so that the mockery on his face seemed to add to his seriousness:

'Underneath are the everlasting arms, don't you know!'

He might have been laughing at pietism, or he might have been laughing at his—the newt's—impertinence for supposing a god or supernatural power minded very much one way or the other what did happen to any little newt in his pond.

That was his way of being superstitious, on which I have already remarked. He never would be definite: left it hanging in the air. Take it or leave it. How shall I put it? Rather as though there *were* a wind, if you kept your sails taut and had a direction.

§ 4

Well, the weather was all right. Hot. Hot sun in a cloudless sky. No wind. A perfect day for a game of cricket. One of the few days on which you knew it could not rain—even in England.

I went down in the morning to have a look at the ground. It looked very nice. The square, larger than ever this year, tightly mown up to the hedge by the road: the outfield cropped: the marquee up: the flag fluttering on the pavilion: rows of chairs for the gentry who would be rolling up in cars during the afternoon for tea.

A man was carting away the cut grass from the long field. All was waiting sleepily expectant. I had a sudden pang to realize how much I should hate to be playing for the last time; and I remembered how many hundred times old Gauvinier had mown the ground himself with a huge machine, a friend and a borrowed pony. I could not get the fellow out of my mind. It seemed more than ever important that this game should at any rate be a really good game: hard fought, with a decent finish. The glorious uncertainty of cricket is all very well in its place; but if the game were a fizzle as some games are, if there were nothing *to* it . . . and I went through in my mind all the infinite varieties possible to a game of cricket: nervous as a kid. Our bowling was fairly sound: so was our batting—better than it had been for quite a few years. Oh hang it! we ought to put up a good show, though the General usually had two or three men who could collar any bowling.

I went to the *Black Rabbit* for a glass of beer, and found that I was not alone in my nervous excitement. Sid Smith was there, on his way home from work; about the only man who had played in the team as long as Gauvinier. He'd lived in the village pretty well all his life. He was full of it.

'I wouldn't half give something for that feller to make a few. Get going. But he'll be that nervous. I know. Too mad keen. . . . Muck himself out. . . .'

I went round to the bar-parlour. More excitement. We were giving him a small presentation: there was heated talk when to give it to him: at the tea interval or after the game—where to give it him—how to give it him. There was, too, considerable anxiety as to whether it would arrive in time.

I heavily vetoed tea-time. It would put him off his game completely: he might have to bat just after tea.

'Well, as soon as the game's over he'll slip off. You know what he is.'

'We can see he doesn't.'

Some wanted the presentation made as publicly as possible on the steps of the pavilion, because everyone who had subscribed would want to see the show: others wanted the thing done as privately as possible—to spare the beggar's feelings—in the small dressing-room of the pavilion, just among the players only. I planked for privacy, and as the talk got heated, went. I found it extraordinarily moving how very, very decent people can be on occasions like this. Freddie Winthrop, for instance, who had enough bother, as I knew, at his home to fill in a lot of overtime, had been giving his mind and time to this presentation, as though he had nothing else to occupy either.

§ 5

I was on the ground early and helped Bliss to open up the shutters of the pavilion. He had already put the screen up by the road. The whole ground was simply smiling in the still sunshine. Sam Bird turned up earlier than usual in his best suit in honour of the game. I helped him rummage the stumps out of the locker, and strolled out into the hot sun to watch him ceremoniously knock them into the ground. It looked a fairly decent wicket, in spite of the dry spell.

'I see,' said old Sam meditatively, 'our worthy skipper has not yet put in an appearance. He's usually here by now.'

'I expect he doesn't want to be hanging about too much before the game begins. Rather awkward in a way.'

'Ah!' said Sam, and shook his head slowly and sadly. 'Most all-firedly awkward, the whole business, if you ask me!'

Players began to turn up—Ballard, Jimmie Harrison, Jack (our spot boy), and Freddie Winthrop, who hoped that Ted Griffith, who worked at a distance, would manage to be in time.

'This lot always turn up to the tick. Blessed if that isn't the first car-load of 'em now. Where's our old bloke? Stuck on the road with a puncture, likely as not. Fuming. What a life!'

He laughed, anxious and ill at ease.

'Take more'n a puncture to keep him from a game of cricket.'

More of the visitors arrived. Paget-Wilson, young Farringdon and old Farrindon (like him to turn up, though he was not able to play). The old skipper was there: these had played in every match since the series started: gave the side its character. There were other familiar faces, and some new ones, but I was glad not to see among them their Spofforth and to hear this year they were weak in bowling. 'After the first two . . .' the old skipper said, and laughed despair. 'However, our batting's sound and we've a first-class stumper. Also I intend to win the toss.'

I was looking out for Gauvinier, couldn't help it somehow, but I didn't see him arrive. I saw him now, walking out across the ground. I thought he was coming to join us. But he waved a cheery greeting to the old skipper and walked on to meet (I turned my head to see) Sid Smith. He put his hand on Sid's shoulder: they shook hands: I didn't hear what they said. The slight unusualness of the little incident hit me sharply. But it was the only sign, and hardly noticeable.

Gauvinier joined us, laughing: explaining the crucial nature of the present game in the series to the old skipper, who could scarcely credit it.

'The ninth game! So many as that! I suppose it must be. Well, it's a jolly good job, then, that I'm going to win the toss.'

'Call and see!' laughed Gauvinier, tossing the coin.

'A head!'

'Of course it is! And we'll bat.'

As they walked off I heard him lower his voice to say to Gauvinier:

'This bad news. I hope it's not true.'

'True enough and foul. Better not think of it.'

And he hurried off to tell the team the toss had been lost and they must take the field. He came hurrying back, however, in a moment to say:

'Tea, I suppose, when it's ready and draw at seven. Good. Or half-past six, if there's nothing to it.'

§ 6

As Tillingfold went out into the field, there were already more spectators on the ground than are wont to watch an ordinary game. The band too were arriving in their neat uniforms—an impressive sight. There were even a sprinkling of gentry on their allotted chairs, giving life to a stretch of the ground, usually deserted except by small boys who, if the game on the square lagged, would start their own in that far corner.

The field was set: the batsmen were making their way to the wicket.

And the game began.

I watched from start to finish, often using glasses. Since then I have been through it time and again with old Gauvinier. I believe I remember every ball bowled in that game: what with watching it with an intensity of keenness: what with discussing it, wicket by wicket, you know, Gauvinier and I, with the score-book on our knees. Nothing comes back in every detail with such peculiar vividness as some games of cricket.

Ballard started the bowling with Gauvinier: a maiden over

each. I was sitting on a bench by the hedge behind Gauvinier's arm and noticed with glee that he was bowling well: once he had his man guessing, once shaved the off stump. Tillingfold are always a keen fielding side—this afternoon they were trembling on the tips of their toes: simply tugging at the leash: a good sight. Dick Culvert at point stretched out and stopped a beauty.

In Ballard's second over his fourth ball jumped in from the off, hit the batsman's glove: Gauvinier ran five yards, stretched a long arm out, got his fingers to it and no more, and dropped as pretty a catch as anyone might like to hold. It was good to have reached it; another couple of inches and he would have held it. Poor old blighter! and every man on the field was sick as mud for him: they wanted him to come off. You could see it.

Runs began to come, all from one man, who had a good shot past cover, just out of young Jack's reach, and a better shot to leg, clean off the leg stump. The runs came off Gauvinier, though he was bowling decently, three twos and a one. Ballard bowled two maiden overs to the man Gauvinier had missed, who seemed in no hurry to open his score. He didn't poke about: he often hit the ball quite hard: but it always went to a fieldsman.

Gauvinier spoke to Ted Griffith, who urged him to keep on bowling; but he told me afterwards he was too dog-tired to bowl: his legs nearly gave way under him from lack of sleep.

He went mid-on and Freddie Winthrop took Ted Griffith's place at mid-off and long-leg. In his next over Ballard put down a beauty, which came in a foot from the off and removed the leg-bail. The outgoing batsman had made all the runs.

16—1—16.

A really good batsman had been beaten by a really good ball, and Redman, although he had made no runs yet, was obviously full of runs and full of confidence too after his good luck. The sort of fellow who seems to be scratching cheerfully round and is really digging himself quietly in: blandly sure that there is no hurry.

Paget-Wilson came in next: one of the cleanest hitters I have ever seen. He has often taken the deuce of a lot of runs off us. He has an astonishing eye: he plays very little cricket, and for the first few balls is shaky, but he has only to feel a couple or so nicely on the bat and it all comes back and the boys are busy with the score-board.

'It's a treat to watch this bloke bat,' Ted Griffith said to Gauvinier. 'I hate to see him get out. I do, straight. He's the prettiest bat as has ever played on this ground. Lovely.'

'Well, yes. That's true. But still . . .'

'I don't mind losing. If someone's got to make the runs . . .'

'This time anyhow. Let's see the back of him.'

'Mind you! of course I'll do my best to get him out.'

Ted Griffith is shortish, and bowls a surprisingly fast ball which is apt to get up quickly. There was no sign as he bowled his first ball of any altruistic intention to encourage an exhibition of delightful batting. His face looked fierce as after a gentle run he flung himself with sudden venom into his de-livery. A good-length ball, bail high, just off the leg stump— a perfect beast for a first one if you happen to be a bit out of practice. Paget-Wilson stopped it somehow, not liking it at all and saying so, so that those within hearing laughed. Everyone liked him immensely. His good humour was so in-fectious that it would be difficult to imagine an unpleasant incident occurring in any game in which he was playing. Some men are like that.

The next ball, shorter and if anything faster, he was glad to jump back from and not touch. There was a smile on Ted's grim little face. The next was a yorker, which Paget-Wilson smothered, pleased, as though there were hope for him yet if he could come down in time on a brute like that. But his luck was dead out, for the fourth ball came sizzling in from the off, hit his glove and was nicely caught by Ballard at short slip. The cries of 'Bad luck, sir,' were genuine.

Ted came up grinning to Gauvinier, and said combatively, 'You mayn't believe it. But I am sorry to see that bloke go.'

Gauvinier did not argue about it: he knew too well what Ted meant.

17—2—0.

And if it hadn't been for a missed catch, 17—3, but it was no good thinking of that, though I know Gauvinier did.

Young Farringdon came in next: he'd been pouching a nice little bag of runs in cricket about a class better than ours, for clubs whose A teams we played. He opened strongly, putting Ted away to leg and driving him: he watched Ballard, however, not liking his break and change of pace. Redman too began to score more freely. The score mounted, though neither batsman took the least liberty.

Gauvinier rested, went on again for Ted, whose shock attack was exhausted, and changed from mid-on to slips. His first over was a maiden: two balls beat Redman and missed the wicket. You could see the old beggar was simply pining to hit the stumps again. Young Farringdon took one off Ballard's first ball, and off the next Redman flicked the ball straight into Gauvinier's hands at short slip. The ball hit him on the chest and fell to the ground without apparently touching his hands at all. I stared, sick at heart. He's usually good at slip. I've seen him hold some real beauties. I knew how he must be feeling. Too dismal.

He bowled too good balls, then two long hops, smitten for a couple each, an half-volley on the leg, swept for four. Not his day. He went back to mid-on. Ted bowled again.

Yet the whole side were more on their toes than ever. Their keenness increased. Dick Culvert at point, always good, had never fielded better—Freddie Winthrop, Jimmie Harrison, Alec John, young Jack and Sid Smith—it was a pleasure to watch them. Upon my soul, you could feel their sickness at the skipper making a fool of himself. A passenger is he to-day? All right, we're glad to take him along as a passenger. You could swear their manner showed some such trend of thought; and as I say, it was a pleasure to watch their work in the field.

Old Gauvinier noticed at any rate. He told me so. Said he was almost glad he'd come such a mucker that day; but that was going a little too far: two catches dropped, and the worst over he'd ever bowled. No, no. That was a bit too thick.

'Proves that I was blear-eyed and knock-kneed, anyhow? Useless by myself: physically useless?'

I agreed to that. I should have even without his almost terrifying insistence upon it.

And runs came. Redman, let off twice, scored faster than young Farringdon, who slowed down. He never potters and pats, but plays hard each shot, as the fieldsmen to whom his shots went noticed: especially Jimmie Harrison and Alec John.

Thirty went up: forty went up. It looked as though these two were in for a big stand, as they neared the fifty, when Ballard, who was keeping a lovely length and having foul luck (not to mention the two dropped catches) in shaving the stumps, got home at last with his fast one, that nipped in from the off and smashed up young Farringdon's wicket, to a roar of applause.

48—3—10.

The lull that follows a new man's entry lasted longer than usual. The batting slowed down. It was a case of Pull devil, pull baker, for the new man got most of the bowling and he remained a dark horse. The sort of fellow that might have surprises up his sleeve. I couldn't place him.

Jimmie Harrison had a swollen finger and couldn't hold the ball to bowl. Ted was keeping a good length; but one wanted a wicket to fall, for Ballard's luck was dead out, though he was bowling beautifully; and then off one of Ted's few really bad balls, a shocking long hop to leg, Alec John brought off a pretty catch, and the new man, so far as I was concerned, remained a dark horse. But anyhow, I was glad to see the back of him.

59—4—4.

Followed in the son of a man who had played first-class cricket in his day, a bowler with an action as perfect as that of Barnes, and who, like Barnes, continued to bowl; he had on one occasion run through our side for a song. The son was a sound bat, awfully well trained you could see at once at a good public school, and as good a fieldsman as you could wish to see. Style and tradition marked every shot. He knew the state of the game, and left it to Redman to make the runs: and Redman made them. He was batting with perfect freedom and confidence, when he stepped to drive Ted Griffith, was a shade late, and drove the ball hard back into the bowler's hands—a lovely catch which made Ted grin with pleasure, and the spectators shout their joy, and it was a good shout, for by now half the village were on the ground.

And the band, in full blast, was playing a mournful dance.

73—5—34.

And seventy-three took some making on our ground, where the length of the grass turned many a good four into two or a miserable one. Old Gauvinier was staring at the score-board—34 and missed twice before he scored five.

Father and son were batting together now, and young Jack was bowling in place of Ballard, who had bowled unchanged till then beautifully, but with infernal luck. This first over was a maiden, but the boy in his second over, seeing that his father was a bit shaky and feeling that he'd better start making some runs (he'd got a nasty bang, too, off Ted in the preceding over), let drive at one on his legs, but not coming out quite far enough lofted it and was neatly caught by Ballard, who had taken young Jack's place at deep mid-wicket.

78—6—6.

Two wickets fell quickly, clean-bowled, the first by young Jack, the second by Ted; and the spectators showed by their cheers that they thought the innings as good as finished. 82 for 8.

I wasn't so sure. A tutor who often went in first when we played the College—the very devil of a man to shift—was batting; and I didn't like the look of Number ten who strode in to join him, the first-class stumper we had heard mentioned: a tall and powerful fellow. He shaped horribly well at his first few balls; but the tutor got most of the bowling for a little while, and was playing with extreme caution, proving to me that Number ten was a hitter. They each took a single to leg off Ted, who was bowling really well, when it came— two quick little steps forward, a lash, and Number ten watched the ball soaring over my head into the road for six: well over the road but not into the pond; it was thrown back from the tea-garden opposite. The last ball was driven into the deep for one; and he had the bowling again. He wasted no time, two twos, both fours but for the grass, and a one, and Ted began to wonder whether another six was coming. It wasn't. Only a four, off a long hop, into the far corner of the field by the swings. Ted's face was a study. The hit had put the hundred up. Every run now was of vital importance. A hundred takes some getting on our ground, unless you've got the bowlers simply addled. Ted lammed them in, and off his last ball Dick Culvert brought off a clinking catch at point— jumping to a hard square cut and holding it.

102—9—18.

But it wasn't over yet. The old skipper started hitting like a two-year-old, though he couldn't run like one, and Ballard was put on for young Jack; and off the third ball of his second over, Dick Culvert had an easy one, straight into his hands. But the score had crept up and the innings closed for 111: leaving Tillingfold 112 to make to win; not much more than two hours to make them in, as tea was always a superb affair on these occasions, topped with ices.

But they'd be going out again before tea, which would be latish.

§ 7

Out was dragged the roller: far too light. They were beginning to bump a bit. Perhaps it was better than nothing.

Yes. Here they were coming out, Paget-Wilson laughing and ragging the skipper as usual.

Who was Gauvinier sending in first? Ah! good. Dick Culvert and Jimmie Harrison.

My Heavens! That innings. I shall never forget it. I wish I could give you any idea of the feeling, pitched higher than a revivalist meeting at its most electric. Anyhow, we should have been made to win this crucial match in the series: especially as we hadn't lost a match during the whole season. And somehow the old beggar's leaving put an edge on the excitement. It would be too stupid to make a presentation after our first defeat of the year, stupider still if we made no show of it at all, and were just skittled idiotically out. I tell you, the intensity of it became pretty well unbearable. These things, you know, are cumulative.

Gauvinier himself fidgeted about less than he usually does at the opening of an innings. He was about through, he looked it, as he stood by the car, talking to his womenfolk, seated inside. Doing a little sum in his mind—111—34: and praying that he might not have to go in a minute or two before the tea-interval. Plus 9 hit off that last foul over of his.

Well, anyhow, there were 112 to get now.

Young Farringdon started the bowling from the elm-tree to Dick Culvert. However well you may know his trick of running up as though he were going to send a fast one, and then stiffening his arm to send down one that infernally hangs, you've got to watch him like a lynx, especially at first, or he will catch you in two minds. And every now and then comes one that doesn't hang.

You could see Dick Culvert holding himself in not to play too soon: his muscles were stiff with restraint, but he got on top of it nicely. The next one was a mistake on the leg-side; no need to stiffen about that one: nor did Dick. He let him have it joyously full and free, a watched four but for the thick grass. However, Jimmie Harrison, running like a deer, insisted on three.

Jimmie Harrison plays his own game: he dislikes nonsense. He has wrists of steel, a wonderful eye, and never wastes time. Along came the ball elaborately made to hang; he waited for it, found it shortish and square-cut it angrily for two.

It was good of course to see runs coming quickly, but the sapient prayed that Dick and Jimmie would be careful. It would be fatal to try and take the slightest liberty with either bowler, yet or for some time.

Vereker was bowling from the road end, his action high and easy as Barnes: still so good that you would like every boy, keen on bowling, to watch it, just to see how it should be done. But it would be impossible that he could bowl for long: medium pace, came in sharp off the pitch: very slight variation of pace: looked nice and innocuous and could be deadly: had it in his bones, the beggar, what to do with the ball: could just flick the bails off. . . .

Tall Dick Culvert reached forward to him, played the ball perfectly back: the same with the next one to mid-on. Then a single and I could see how Jimmie would shape to Vereker. As I feared, he waited for him and played back at the last second, a queer shot of his own, with a quick flick from the wrists. Vereker was obviously pleased: must beat him or get him caught at the wicket or in the slips. For any other man it would have been a certainty. Jimmie's shot, however, is his own. The next he hit to point, who was glad to stop it, and the next well past point for a couple. How he does it is his secret. But well as I knew Jimmie's play, it frightened me to see him use that shot with Vereker. And if ever a man was nearly bowled, Jimmie was by two of the next three balls. The bails fairly shivered on the stumps: my inside trembled with them. However, Jimmie was still in, and quite unperturbed cut him again for two in his next over. It is such a last-second shot that it is painful to watch when runs are of vital importance.

And both Jimmie and Dick were being too contemptuous of young Farringdon. They helped themselves to six more off his next over to misplaced yells of joy. And then Dick played every ball of an over from Vereker steadily, carefully and well, except one ball which bumped and made him feel foolish. No small boy yelled with joy, but the hearts of the judicious glowed with pleasure: a few overs played like that would do far more to win the match.

Jimmie believed in runs; and kept on the merry work with young Farringdon, tanking him for two—then driving him for a single far into the slow deep. Dick faced him: was morally certain that the next one must be the fast one: and morally speaking it certainly ought to have been, but it wasn't. Dick, miles too soon for it, patted up, as he was intended to do, a dolly catch to the gloating bowler, and retired cursing himself for having fallen into such an obvious trap.

19—1—9.

Quite a decent start, but it looked as though it were going to be far better.

In marched Alec John, wearing, for some good Scottish reason, a beautiful red cap, to show possibly that they do play cricket in that strange land across the Border. He put young Farringdon away immediately for a hard-hit one to deep mid-wicket, who by his speed saved two. It would have been better for Jimmie had he risked the second run as he badly wanted to (only a strange Hieland shout succeeded in sending him back), for he took a happy dip at the next ball and, completely baffled by the pace, was bowled, another victim of that perpetually set trap.

20—2—10.

Two good men out: a quarter of an hour and more to go before tea: young Farringdon above himself, as any bowler would be who had got two wickets, precisely as he wanted to get them, in one over. Ballard came in, our best bat: missed the last ball of the over completely, but it was well off the wicket, luckily.

Alec could make little of Vereker; he hadn't the reach to play properly forward to his good-length ball. He took a half-cock shot at the last ball, and was nicely caught at cover. A full hit, and he would have got hold of it, as well he knew, coming out frowning, and beating his pad with his bat: just near enough to bad luck to make any batsman furious, being even nearer to merely foolish play.

Things were beginning to look serious, for the score-board read:

24—3—2.

Ted Griffith came in. He and Ballard, together now, were pretty well our last hope. Young Jack, getting his pads on, hadn't been making runs: Gauvinier—well, he wasn't himself, and after him no one who could make runs, though one or two could keep up their wicket, especially Freddie Winthrop.

Ten fateful minutes at least before the tea interval. Ted and Ballard knew well their responsibility and rose to it. They played good sound cricket, taking no shadow of a risk, hitting the loose ones hard and clean.

And then at last the signal for tea was given. Ted 9 not out, Ballard 7 not out, and the score 39. We were still deep in the wood, but there was a faint chance of winning, if those two got going as they well might, after tea.

§ 8

Oh, it seemed an interminable meal, that tea. I'd finished my flask and biscuits long before there was a sign of anyone emerging from the tent. Then one came, puffing out the smoke from a cigarette, then another, lounging about, talking, in the air.

Gauvinier came striding out, making for his car. I knew how he was feeling, strung up to snapping. He met old Farringdon, and stopped to talk. Young Farringdon joined them.

'When are you going in?' the old fellow asked him.

'Number seven,' said Gauvinier.

'Good place for the skipper.'

'Yes,' young Farringdon said. 'You've pulled a good many games out of the fire from Number seven in your time, haven't you?'

'I'll watch our friend here do it to-day perhaps.'

'Not to-day. I'm afraid not.'

'Not if I know it!' laughed young Farringdon, making off for the pavilion.

The umpires went out again: the solemnity of the occasion written large upon Sam Bird's expansive face. . The fieldsmen took their places: cheers rose for the batsmen. Ted wore his grim grin of intention: a short chap, very shy, who walked boldly like a tall man. Ballard, dark as a Spaniard, half as tall again, assumed the air of nonchalance. If you knew anything, you knew that each in his own way was keyed up to the very last peg of resolution to pull the side through on this the last lap of the great match. Men as different as two men could well be, yet one for the moment in this their common desire. And anyone who happened to like to see men at their best rejoiced at the sight.

Old cricket worthies (and there were a goodish few of them on the ground), too old to play now, still just able on a warm day to watch, saw them walk out with a sharp pang, remembering times in their own young days when they had gone out to bat on an occasion like this and perhaps they had made them, remembering such times with a vividness past all belief, so that to be sitting disabled by age on a bench seemed the preposterous foolish illusion.

But the bowler was about to deliver his first ball, Ballard was standing ready to play it, the fieldsmen stood alert—we all forgot ourselves (the old men even their age-brought disabilities) in the interest of the present game, which closed down upon us and held us, taking us into itself.

Gauvinier looked at the old men watching, looked at the young men playing . . . *actum est de* will always contain its knell of sadness, in great affairs or small: whether it is all up with the Roman Republic or your little games of cricket, my boy. They became absorbed. We all became absorbed in the game.

Redman was bowling, not Vereker. That was interesting: his bowling was new to us. There didn't seem much in it. Ballard at any rate played him with perfect ease, and seemed to see him all the way. I noticed Vereker moving his right shoulder up, patting it, as though to make sure whether it was mere stiffness or a strain.

They ran a single. Ted found no difficulty either with Redman, pushed him back to mid-off as though he'd been playing him for a week. One settled back with some small sense of relief: not too much, as horrid accidents may happen.

But young Farringdon was the main danger: that trap of his, however obvious, was likely to prove fatal to any batsman, strung up and a little over-eager. But Ballard was fully aware of his guile, watched and waited and was quite content with a single. Ted, too, kept a tight hand on his impatience and played the last two balls back along the ground with a good straight bat, and no hesitation.

Slowly and well, they were settling down. And then one thing became apparent—namely, that the man who had remained a dark horse in the batting and who was fielding third man to Redman (in the deep, on the leg-side to young Farringdon) was an exceptionally brilliant fieldsman. Ballard cut a short one hard in his direction, and he, having watched it on to and off the bat, ready for the shot, reached it, and then in one good swift action gathered it and threw it in bail-high to the stumper. The next ball, too, would have been a safe two to an ordinary man; only a sharp and timely shout from Ballard, sending Ted back, saved the loss of an all-important wicket.

Ted made it all right for himself by beating the next ball hard past cover, his first good happy hit since tea. Two only, not four as it should have been! Young Farringdon was bowling well: not the semblance of a loose ball came as a little gift to Ballard, who would not be hurried and helped himself to a pretty two with a square cut past point.

Then quite suddenly the whole of the game underwent a complete change. Redman, practically for the first time, got by the batsman, though not at all near the wicket. Whether this made Ted angry or the bowler above himself, I don't know, but all the remaining five balls of that over, Ted lashed between the covers for twos, and Redman bowled no more. The applause was furious. The score was mounting. There remained young Farringdon, but they were taking his measure, stepping out and driving him for long deep hits, that only scored one very likely, but were significant.

The old skipper went on in place of Redman. He very rarely bowled now; but he knew exactly what he wanted to do with the ball, though he was not always quite able to do it. He was a cricketer, through and through. He was bowling from the road end to Ballard, who watched him carefully. He was nearly stumped, too, off the second ball: the bail whipped off but no appeal. Not the ghost of a liberty could be taken with that stumper behind the wicket. And then out came Ballard to the fifth ball and lifted it hard and true. Clean over the road for six. The effect of that hit on the game was greater than the six runs recorded in the score-book, and in the next over after Ted had put young Farringdon to leg for a single, Ballard hit him through the covers for a couple and then lifted him into the hedge for four.

When at the end of that over we saw young Farringdon in earnest conversation with the old skipper, who gazed round to see whom he could put on to bowl, even the most sapient felt a glow of confidence, for if ever two men could paste loose bowling, Ballard and Ted were those men, and, moreover, they were well set and seeing the ball to perfection. We were well out of the wood: hardly a bush in sight: clear open country: easy going. In the last few minutes the score had jumped from the early forties to well over sixty. I could scarcely believe my eyes when I looked at my watch to see that it was barely a quarter to six; so much had happened in so short a time. There was no ghost of a need for any hurry. The clock at any rate was now beaten. It was all right about Gauvinier: no call would be made upon him now—he'd have a quiet knock and our presentation would end the game nicely. Everything was panning out perfectly.

And oh, my sacred Aunt, write home to tell the glad tidings to mother, Paget-Wilson was going slip in place of young Farringdon. Paget-Wilson, whose bowling was his friend, the old skipper's, stock joke! Ballard, after the confabulation about the new bowler, now faced the old skipper, and we all got ready to applaud another six into the road.

But it didn't come. Something very different came: totally unexpected: something that made you stare and gape in angry amazement, confounded, for Ballard, as sound a cricketer as any I have seen on the ground, Ballard cut the ball hard to third man, no longer a dark horse in the field, and galloped down the wicket like a silly prep. school kid, to Ted yelling him to get back. Third man picked up the ball and flung it back in one swift clean action, hard into the hands of the stumper, who nipped off the bails with Ballard wandering like a lost soul yards outside the crease. No appeal, no decision. Poor Ballard simply made his way back to the pavilion—to a storm of applause of course for his magnificent knock: which he hardly seemed to notice, lost as he was in bewilderment at his unprecedented foolishness.

67—4—22.

Young Jack came in, who can hit as hard, if not harder, than any man in the team: a terror to a tired bowler, a fiend on a loose ball. But his luck was out this season. However, this was a good day to turn his luck in the right direction.

Oh Lord, but that won't do; he took a blind swipe at his first ball, and was nowhere near it. The stumper whipped off the bail too; but again there was no appeal, though it must have been a pretty near thing.

Excitement came welling back; tingling, painful. And now Paget-Wilson took the ball to bowl to Ted, who could hit with sudden concentrated fury.

Paget-Wilson took a short uncomfortable run and delivered the ball as though he needed all his body's strength to get his arm over at all. Bowling looked an extremely difficult and arduous feat. His first ball was wide, which slip moved to the right to reach. His next was a slow painful toss within the batsman's reach and Ted banged it into the hedge for four. The next bumped down almost at his own feet and rolled along the ground. The fourth was a ball that could be played: the fifth was not given a wide. The sixth was another slow easy full toss . . . waste time over fours—over the blasted hedge—but he missed the ball completely, and the slow full toss slowly knocked down his wicket.

It was a more amazing sight than Ballard's run out. I have never before—never—often as I have watched Ted at the nets or batting in a game, seen him completely miss such a ball.

71—5—22.

Once more the whole character of the game had changed. Forty-one more runs were needed: and the two set batsmen had been fooled out. There was young Jack, true. . . .

And Gauvinier was walking in. Damned if I could look in his direction. There came suppressed clapping, suppressed, yet eager: aching to cheer him: fearful of putting him off his game.

I looked up to see him taking his block. Young Farringdon went back to slip. I could hardly force myself to look at the first ball. I couldn't bear to see his stumps disarranged or a silly little catch hit up off the first ball. Still I had to look. Do you know, I said aloud, 'Oh, thank God!' when he hit that first ball clean and true for an easy single. Then one for young Jack: and he had the bowling again. A long hop on the off—he's got it, got it with all his strength, it'll reach the boundary, must—damn that accursed thick grass—but they've run three. My heavens! it was good to hear the yell of delight which greeted that shot. Pent up, my God! and then we had a chance to let it loose. It was let loose. See him striding between the wicket with those long legs, using every inch of his length to spare his wind. If he and young Jack got going we should be all right.

But young Jack took a tremendous whack at the next ball, blind certain of a six; the bat was a fraction of an inch out of place: hit the ball a shade on the edge, and up it went higher and higher, a huge height into the air, and underneath stood Vereker, moving with unhurrying stride to the exact spot where it must fall, and did fall into his safe hands.

I must have missed some shots in my excitement, for I thought the score-board must be wrong in displaying the figures.

84—6—1.

I went into the box to consult old Francis, who was past speech of any kind, in his frantic anxiety that Gauvinier should make runs: he muttered unprintable appellations. He was rather keen on Gauvinier. So was I. I cleared out. But everywhere there was the same intensity of feeling. Unbearable. I almost wished the old swine *had* got out first ball and not be keeping us hanging on tenterhooks—waiting, looking, hoping. At any rate we should have been done with it.

Freddie Winthrop came hurrying out, sworn to keep his end up. These two had made many a decent stand together. Would they once more? Judging by his set face, it wouldn't be Freddie's fault if they didn't.

The next ten minutes were agonizing: the tenseness of the rope when two exactly balanced teams are straining at the pull. A sort of vibrant stillness in which Gauvinier's voice sounded loud, calling after every ball, *No* or *Wait*, for he says something at every ball bowled, old-fashioned perhaps but right, dead right. Only ones came, and those slowly. The old skipper took himself off, spoke to Vereker, who moved his arm up and down, decided it was mostly stiffness, not a strain, and went on to bowl.

He bowled Gauvinier a maiden. I suppose the delivery of six balls can only last an allotted time; but they seemed to last an eternity, though Gauvinier seemed to be seeing them perfectly, and using his reach without any hesitation. Two singles came off Farringdon's next over, each loudly applauded. The score crawled up. And there followed another long, long maiden to Gauvinier. I could not believe my eyes to see him playing, thus patiently, without flurry, like a good example from a good book; but the strain of watching it was terrible. Two singles and a two off Farringdon, and each run was cheered like a six: men were walking up and down in their excitement: wiping their faces: scratching themselves: pommelling each other like little boys: it was ridiculous to see.

And once more Gauvinier was standing ready for Vereker. And look! a wild roar burst from every man as we saw the ball rise . . . the man in the deep stepping back, stop at the hedge, and the ball bounce in the road and up again so that Gauvinier saw it on the bounce, over the hedge: a little high for a perfectly safe six but a glorious smack. Motor horns hooted; men kept on shouting; a little girl by their car waved her arms about madly. Stillness for the next ball: played quietly back. Then a bad long hop. Gauvinier withdrew and with all his might smote it into the hedge, well out of reach of the man in the deep: another roar of joy went up.

Damnation! the old beggar was going to pull it off after all, was he?

Sid Smith called out: 'And just once more, please!' and everyone burst out laughing. Vereker was taken off; changed places with the old skipper.

Freddie, after a leg-bye, took a couple off him; that sent up the hundred. Twelve more, by Gum! But there came another halt: a single here, a single there. Neither bowler gave anything away. And then Freddie, trying to smother a straight one, got right in front of his wicket and was out l.b.w.

105—7—5.

Sam Gault came in. Four more runs, and Sam was stumped.

109—8—1.

Then Sid Smith came out to join his skipper, stooping on

his way to pick a bent for chewing to a shout of laughter. Hit the last ball of the over for two. It was a tie.

You should have heard the yell that greeted Gauvinier's next shot off young Farringdon, as good a drive as he has ever made, far past extra-cover—into the thickest of thick grass. He was shaking all over after running that three—the winning hit. It was twenty minutes past six.

They went on playing. We talked and laughed, at perfect ease at last, all strain gone. Soon Sid patted up a catch to Vereker, and came running out. Charlie came in for a knock, and while he was still in, the umpire called out last over.

Lord God! how Gauvinier was cheered. Some were for carrying him in. We flocked round him.

He rushed off to his womenfolk—jumped on to the running-board, leaned into the car, shaking hands, saying, 'What did I tell you? Still going strong?'

He came back: he was pouring with sweat—panting, shaking—to take off his pads. Old Francis called out, 'Forty not out. And not too bad for you, metty.'

A small boy helped him take his pads off; his hands were shaking. Dick Culvert stood by him.

'I'm going to slip off now.'

'Yes, just a minute.'

He took him by the arm and guided him to the small changing room. All the team were there. They started shaking hands with him. There was hardly room to move— such a tight little packed crowd. He was pushing out, when the General began to speak and we all crowded back to make some small gap. Gauvinier sat down, bewildered, still sweating, bowed his head.

The General spoke slowly and with genuine feeling. Of what Gauvinier had done for the cricket, of his example of sportsmanship—all the familiar things, you know: but none of them sounded in the least familiar under the circumstances.

Gauvinier, right in the thick of it as it were, bowed his head lower and lower. The General stopped and presented the silver inkstand, which Gauvinier stood holding.

He began to speak in reply: began very well—'All these pleasant things said . . . but of course it's the fellows one plays with make the game. . . .' Then he stopped suddenly, swallowed. His face puckered: he managed to articulate 'Thank you very much,' and burst out at the little changing-room door, clutching the inkstand.

That's the story of the game.

'If it had been arranged for me,' Gauvinier said, 'it could not have been more perfect. All I wanted. To hit a six. To have another little stand with Freddie and Sid: to come off— and I was physically beaten: too knock-kneed to bowl—too blear-eyed to see. Do you see what I mean?' I did in a way. But the fact is that he is superstitious, and superstitious in a way that I don't really very much like. But, dear God! How he treasures that inkstand!

OURS IS THE REAL CRICKET!

(*To Fred Humphrey*)

In memory of the little shield you gave me to protect my watch and of the best wickets that were ever prepared on the ground and were prepared by you.

THEY say that village cricket is not what it was. In old days there was never any difficulty about the ground, all the lads were keen and courteous, little boys never scrimmaged into the pavilion, hot grog was sold to spectators during the game, the side made itself up each week without a hitch, the batting was steady and vastly superior, and, above all, what is quite out of the question nowadays, young fellows could be taught. Halcyon days, obviously; quite the golden age.

Moreover, I have often been told, a cricket match then was far more of a high day and holiday than it is now. No one ever dreamed of leaving the ground before dark. Oh, no! When the proper game was over, old Sam or old Joe, or someone or t'other would be sure to challenge a pal for a match at single-wicket, for a wager, you understand. A deep, reminiscent chuckle, then: 'That 'ud be a bit o' fun and no mistake. They'd be three parts oiled up by that time, y'see. And not a chap but had a bob on one or t'other.'

Thus old men who used to be famous performers fifty years ago (the *White Horse* boasts a picture of a great game played on ice, one hard winter) wag their heads over these degenerate days. 'No, no. Young fellers don't seem so keen nowadays—not like they waur when I was a nipper. These here pickchers and them motor-cycles flyin' all over the country does 'em no good. Don't tell me! *And* must 'ave everything done for 'em. *And* then it's not good enough. Oh, no! Things is very different from what they was.'

They most assuredly are—very different. For one thing, no hot grog is served on the field. But, naturally, these revered old men never refer to the old fellers who wagged sad heads over *them* in their young days; so we are apt to be left with a rosy picture of the past, by contrast with which the present looks drab and poor and meagre, especially as changes have occurred during the last forty years more drastic and more far-reaching than have ever occurred in the history of man.

Cricket is no longer the only interest during the summer, or, indeed, during the year, since football was seldom played. Accordingly, the difficulties of arranging a side and keeping it together have greatly increased. Also there is a spirit of independence rife among 'young chaps' which is new and good, but does not always express itself to the convenience either of its possessor or of others. *Nemo repente fuit turpissimus*, says the old Latin tag of our schooldays; and nobody either *repente fuit excellentissimus*, for growth is slow, and, as Sam Bird never tires of reminding us (he is our umpire and should know), 'It is an imperfect world, gentlemen, an imperfect world.'

But however great and glorious the past may have been, with its hot grog, and single-wicket matches played for a wager, and its nice compact care-free side, I beg leave to doubt whether better, keener, more sporting games could ever have been played than many I have enjoyed during the last ten years or so; and as I happily brood over these games, remembering that all is now ready for yet one more season, countless incidents leap into my mind that I shall never forget, and no player on either side is likely to forget, though they are unrecorded in Wisden.

We hear so much about the rosy past and how things are not what they were, that it is good (and, I hope, not immodest) to mention a few facts about the present, even though they happen to be rosy. How, for instance, in our club, a boy of fifteen made the first fifty he had ever scored at cricket in the same season as a man of fifty made the first hundred ('faint yet pursuing,' you know) that *he* had ever scored in cricket—a sweet little record that I should like to hear beaten.

Then again: the President of our club brings a fairly warm side against us every year. It is the match of the season. ('And don't those pretty little jackets of theirs put the wind up you all proper,' chuckles our scorer—and no wonder, seeing that they show I Zingari, Authentics, M.C.C., Eton, Wellington, and so forth!) Which of us will ever forget the game when four of our wickets fell for two runs (fell!—knocked spinning, rather, in that deadly fast bowler's first two desolating overs) and how we declared at tea-time with 227 for 7 (our record score) and got them out with three minutes to spare? A game, begad, if ever there was one!

How we beat a rival club by two, three and four in successive seasons and then tied at 143, the bails falling off the last wicket as the clock struck seven, literally on the stroke of time.

Then, too, on the same small perfect ground (last season, alas! the builder spread his horrid tentacles over it) a tall naval lieutenant, who was playing for us, walked quietly in and began to help himself to sixes (forty-four in two overs), leaning forward and lifting ball after ball out of the ground so that the field became paralysed and stood limply on the boundary watching the hits soar over their heads and the mishits drop safely where men should have been standing but weren't. We declared at tea-time ('Lootie' 136) on that unforgettable day with 220 odd on the board. I happened to be playing the following week with a hot scratch side against practically the same team on the same ground. Lootie strolled in, immaculate, waved his bat at the first ball and was bowled by the next. Such is cricket.

But I could go on yarning till the middle of next week—and then some, as Babe Ruth would say. (Baseball! Ye gods and little fishes!) But there is one good fact that clamours for mention; a fact that is true to my knowledge of every village cricket club in Sussex. The County Club, in which we all take a fierce personal pride, is not an aloof place of grandeur on to whose grounds we occasionally creep to watch real class cricket and creep away again, feeling very small and foolish, to our antics on the village green.

Not a bit of it. It is in a very real sense the Parent Club; and we go to Hove or Horsham with our heads up, at our ease and welcomed, to watch and appreciate the finer points of the great game, which are not to be seen with such frequency in our own brighter, shorter and less skilful battles. For the officials are not content with fostering the good spirit of the game among the actual playing members of the county team; they take pains to see that it spreads far and wide throughout the countryside.

How? Pretty well every village club during the winter runs a cricket supper, and representatives from the county accept invitations to these suppers. On one occasion, for instance, Mr. Knowles the secretary, Arthur Gilligan, and Maurice Tate came to our supper in the market room at the pub. Arthur Gilligan made us rock with laughter with tales of Test matches in Australia, and ended up: 'I like this sort of show; I hope you'll ask me again.'

We happened to know that he had driven some thirty miles on a winter's night to come, and had fifty miles to drive on to London after the supper was over; and we have no doubt which is the most sporting side in the country, and no doubt, whatever, *why* it is the most sporting side.

And this policy of the County Club does more, a great deal more, than increase subscriptions and keep alive an interest in the great game. Unostentatiously and surely, with no high-sounding talk or pulling of long, earnest faces, something is generated which takes off from cricket to the even greater game of living, and that something is the spirit of active good-will, the finest and most precious thing in life.

The Cricket Match

Hugh de Selincourt

Introduction by Benny Green

'Hugh de Selincourt's book . . . is delightful, and beautifully distils the essence of a lasting aspect of English village life.' Marghanita Laski, *Country Life*

'It's entertaining and humorous, and the charm is lined with some abrasive ironies. It might even make cricket seem three-dimensional to an outsider. . . ' Alex Hamilton, *Guardian*

'There is a case for asserting that *The Cricket Match* is the best story about cricket, or any other sport, ever written. Even Americans, and other lesser breeds, without the law whose eyes glaze over at the mention of sticky wickets . . . can catch the brilliance of the game from it.' Philip Howard, *The Times*

The Diary of a Georgian Shopkeeper

Thomas Turner

With a new introduction by G. H. Jennings

'I cannot say I came home sober.' Recurrent drunkenness (and attendant guilt) might be called the leading theme of the diary of Thomas Turner of East Hoathly in Sussex, a most candid, perceptive, entertaining personal document with unique social and historical overtones. The subjects Turner touches on are many and very various: his activities as shopkeeper, church warden, and Overseer to the Parish Vestry; the principal historical events of the period (1754–65), with Turner's (often unexpected) reactions to them; reflections on marriage; accounts of his first wife's illness and death, and of his courting of a new wife; the races, cockfighting, cricket; poverty, boredom, illness and death; and of course continual drinking.

Small Talk at Wreyland

Cecil Torr

With a new introduction by Jack Simmons

In 1916 Cecil Torr began to record the character and history of Wreyland, a tiny hamlet on the edge of Dartmoor where he lived. By drawing on the letters and diaries of his father and grandfather, as well as on his own eccentric memory, he provided a chronicle of about 150 years. His aim was to preserve the wealth of local knowledge still retained by the older natives, but he wanders from idea to idea in *Small Talk*, butting in on his own narrative with such words as 'I once spent a night on the summit of Etna. . .'. *Small Talk* is full of fascinatingly incongruous anecdotes, but it is most importantly an exact diary of Devonshire life, correct to the minutest detail. A contemporary reviewer commented in the *New Statesman*: 'I do not know any book in which so many characteristic and uniformly good stories of Devonshire folk are to be found.'

The Adventures of Mr Verdant Green

Cuthbert Bede

Introduction by Anthony Powell

As his name suggests, Mr Verdant Green is a gullible innocent. When he leaves his country home to attend Brazenface College, Oxford, he finds himself the butt of practical jokes, swindles, and hoaxes played on him by more worldly men. His career at the University is the subject of this hilarious comedy, first published between 1853 and 1857, and one of the earliest examples of the 'Oxford novel'. The book is profusely and delightfully illustrated by the author, Edward Bradley, whose pseudonym of Cuthbert Bede is an amalgam of the names of the patron saints of his real Alma Mater, Durham.

A Nursery in the Nineties

Eleanor Farjeon

'Beautifully written . . . vividly evokes the extraordinary
freedom and ease of children's culture in our more advantaged
society.' *The Guardian*

Eleanor Farjeon is probably best known for her powerfully
imaginative children's books, so it is not surprising to discover
that her own childhood was a happy and creative one. In
keeping with the fashion of the day, Nellie, who was born in
1881, was never sent to school, and the only world she knew for
more than sixteen years was in her nursery. It was here that she
read and wrote stories with her three brothers and created a
fantasy world that became more exciting to her than the real
world of Victorian London outside. In *A Nursery in the Nineties*
she describes her early years, and in so doing gives us one of the
most striking accounts of childhood ever written.

English Hours

Henry James

Introduction by Leon Edel

'The great relisher of impressions and nuances turns his attention in these occasional pieces to aspects of English life, metropolitan and provincial. Wonderful.' *Sunday Times*

English Hours is an affectionate portrait, warts and all, of the country that was to become Henry James's adopted homeland. One of the great travel writers of his time, James takes the reader on a series of visits, ranging from Winchelsea to Warwick, taking in abbeys and castles, sea-fronts and race-courses. Though no mere travel guide, the book will certainly enhance any tourist's pleasure.

The Diary of a Country Parson, 1788–1802

James Woodforde

Edited by John Beresford

James Woodforde was parson at Weston Longeville, Norfolk, from 1774 till his death in 1803. His life was obscure and tranquil, his character uncomplicated; he loved his country, sport, good food, and established institutions, and was warm-hearted and generous. His diary covers nearly every single day in his life from 1758 to 1802. What makes it a classic as well as a remarkable document of social history is Parson Woodforde's rare ability to bring vividly to life the rural England of two centuries ago.